THE RAIDING PARTY

"Listen," Zach abruptly said, reining up.

Lou had been so deep in thought, she hadn't heard the faint pop of rifles and pistols. "The settlers! They're under attack!"

Together they broke into a gallop, speeding parallel with the trees, the manes and tails of their horses flying. Zach's bay was capable of outdistancing Lou's mare but he was unwilling to leave her behind.

The *crack-crack-crack* of the guns grew steadily louder.

When they were near enough to hear strident war whoops, Zach veered to the left, into the undergrowth, and slowed to a cautious walk. Another hundred yards brought them within sight of the conflict.

"Land sakes!" Lou declared.

Forty or fifty warriors were taking part in the raid. Some were armed with bows, some with lances, some with war clubs. Only a few had rifles. In constant motion, yipping like frenzied coyotes, they swooped down on the Conestogas. . . .

The *Wilderness* Series:

#1: KING OF THE MOUNTAIN
#2: LURE OF THE WILD
#3: SAVAGE RENDEZVOUS
#4: BLOOD FURY
#5: TOMAHAWK REVENGE
#6: BLACK POWDER JUSTICE
#7: VENGEANCE TRAIL
#8: DEATH HUNT
#9: MOUNTAIN DEVIL
#10: BLACKFOOT MASSACRE
#11: NORTHWEST PASSAGE
#12: APACHE BLOOD
#13: MOUNTAIN MANHUNT
#14: TENDERFOOT
#15: WINTERKILL
#16: BLOOD TRUCE
#17: TRAPPER'S BLOOD
#18: MOUNTAIN CAT
#19: IRON WARRIOR
#20: WOLF PACK
#21: BLACK POWDER
#22: TRAIL'S END
#23: THE LOST VALLEY
#24: MOUNTAIN MADNESS
#25: FRONTIER MAYHEM
#26: BLOOD FEUD
#27: GOLD RAGE
#28: THE QUEST
#29: MOUNTAIN NIGHTMARE
#30: SAVAGES
#31: BLOOD KIN

WILDERNESS

THE WESTWARD TIDE

DAVID THOMPSON

LEISURE BOOKS NEW YORK CITY

To Judy, Joshua, and Shane

A LEISURE BOOK®

December 2000

Published by

Dorchester Publishing Co., Inc.
276 Fifth Avenue
New York, NY 10001

ISBN 0-8439-4812-4

Printed in the United States of America.

THE WESTWARD TIDE

Chapter One

They were young and in love and nothing else mattered.

Zachary King and Louisa May Clark rode side by side along the south bank of the Platte River, the morning sun warm on their backs. In the slender cottonwoods and tall oaks that lined the waterway dozens of birds merrily chirped, while frisky squirrels arced from branch to branch in dizzying leaps. A grazing whitetail doe lifted her head to warily regard them.

Presently, a startled rabbit shot from a patch of undergrowth and bounded off in great leaps. The young couple hardly noticed. They had eyes only for each other, their arms extended, their fingers linked.

Zach King was so happy he could whoop for joy. They were finally on their way home after a harrowing visit to St. Louis. In a month or so they would be back in the Rocky Mountains, back where they belonged, back with his folks and friends. As soon as they got there he would set to work building a cabin, a place of their very own where they would start their own family. He couldn't wait.

Louisa Clark wasn't thinking of their future so much as the immediate past. She knew they had been lucky to get out of St. Louis alive, and it troubled her deeply that her own kin, those who were dearest to her heart, had turned against her and tried to tear her away from the one she loved.

Lou had been aware, of course, that there were those who disliked Zach for no other reason than the accident of his birth. His father was white, his mother a Shoshone. That made him a half-breed. And for reasons she couldn't quite fathom, many whites and Indians alike hated 'breeds. Hated them with a ferocity bordering on madness.

To Lou it made no difference that Zach's mother was an Indian. He was as fine and handsome a man as she had ever met. So what if red blood flowed in his veins? Wasn't *all* blood red, when it came right down to it?

The snort of Zach's bay ended their tender interlude. Facing forward, Zach spotted tendrils of smoke spiraling skyward about a quarter-mile ahead. It was a campfire. Given the amount of smoke, he reasoned that whites were responsible. And as he had so recently been reminded, to his bitter sorrow, whites often spelled trouble. "Let's swing to the south a ways," he suggested.

"Who do you reckon it is?" Lou asked. Her main worry was hostiles. The Arikaras had been acting up of late, and wouldn't hesitate to kill two lone travelers.

"Doesn't matter," Zach said. "I say we play it safe and fight shy of them."

"Whatever you think is best," Lou said, reluctantly letting go of his callused hand. As they reined their mounts, she found herself admiring the square jut of his jaw, his piercing green eyes, his raven-hued braided hair. Like her, he was dressed in buckskins and had a powder horn, ammo pouch, and possibles bag slanted across his chest. Wedged under his wide leather belt were a matched pair of smoothbore flintlock pistols. On his right hip hung a Bowie knife. Across his saddle rested a heavy Hawken rifle.

Lou was likewise armed to the teeth. She had to be. The wilderness swarmed with savage beasts as well as savage men. There were great bears that could rip a person in half with a single swipe of their massive paws. There were painters, as the mountain men called them, enormous cats with razor teeth and claws. There were wolves and buffalo and rattlers and much, much more.

For anyone, man or woman, to traipse around defenseless was a surefire invitation to an early grave. Unlike in a city, where everyone took it for granted everyone else would behave in a fairly civilized fashion, on the frontier, and beyond, the opposite was the case. Everyone was a potential enemy until they proved otherwise.

Zach threaded through the trees to the edge of the grassland. He had not ventured more than ten feet out when rutted tracks greeted his questing gaze. They were fresh, made the day before by wagons filing westward. The ruts overlapped, so it was impossible to tell exactly how many. "A wagon train," he commented, drawing rein. "Most likely bound for the Oregon country."

"My pa was talking about going there after we saved up enough money," Lou remarked, and grew sad. It never failed. Every time she dwelled on her father and his grand plan, on how he had dragged her off to the Rockies to trap beaver to raise the stake they needed, and how their venture had ended in his violent death, her heart felt as if it would rip asunder.

Zach had seen her sorrowful expression before and changed the subject. "Whoever they are, they're leaving too late in the summer. The first snow will hit before they reach the Snake."

Shifting, Lou stared at the smoke. "Maybe we should warn them."

The play of sunlight on her lovely features stirred Zach mightily. He never tired of feasting in the sight of her; Lou's soft, sandy hair, lively lake-blue eyes, pert lips, and winsome form were enough to set his pulse to quickening. "Why bother? They'll only tell us to tend to our own business."

"I suppose," Lou said, and followed when he clucked to his bay. She put the wagon train from her mind and focused on the new life they were carving out for themselves upon their return to the high country. A vision of the cabin they would build floated before her, complete with frilly curtains and a flower garden and a wood shed close by so she wouldn't have to walk far to get firewood on cold winter days.

Zach kept one eye on the smoke. Accordingly, he was first to notice several riders approaching. He considered retreating into the trees, but he could tell the riders had already spotted them. One was pointing and gesturing excitedly. "Looks as if someone wants to palaver," he said, and halted. Turning the bay toward them, he leveled his Hawken.

Louisa imitated his example. She counted three men, all dressed in homespun clothes, all wearing straw-colored hats typical of farmers, and all with rifles. In the lead was a tall broomstick whose hair and thin beard were flecked with streaks of gray. She mustered an uneasy smile.

The trio drew rein half a dozen yards off. They were clearly in an agitated state, made more evident when the older man demanded without preliminaries, "Where is she? Have you seen her?"

"Seen who?" Zach responded. He didn't like how the white man on the right was staring straight at him as if he were a bug worthy of being crushed underfoot. He'd been the recipient of such looks before, and they always rankled him.

"Maybe this 'breed took her, Orville," the man on the right snapped. "Maybe we should haul him off his horse and whittle on him some to make him tell us what he did with her."

Zach bristled at the threat. "I'd like to see you try."

Orville, the older man, glanced sharply at the bigot. "Enough of that kind of talk, Jensen. I've warned you before about that tongue of yours." He looked at Zach and Lou, his anxiety resurfacing. "My granddaughter, Susie Mills, is missing. We figure she wandered off sometime during the night and got lost."

"We've been searching for her since sunup," said the third one, who was in his early twenties. He had a round, full, friendly face. "We're part of a wagon train, you see. Twelve families bound for—"

Jensen cut the younger man off. "Use your head, Baxter. For all we know, he could be shadowing us, waiting for a chance to pick one of us off and rob us. He doesn't deserve to know a blessed thing."

"I'm no robber," Zach declared.

"So you claim" was the bigot's response. "But why else are you following us?"

Orville gave Jensen another searing glance. "Will you stop it? Susie's life is in peril, and all you can think to do is pick a fight? If these two haven't seen her, we've got to keep on looking."

Lou had held her tongue long enough. She disliked Jensen immensely, but she felt keen sympathy for the distraught grandfather. "Have you tried tracking her, mister?" she politely asked.

Orville, about to turn his mount, shook his head. "No, ma'am. None of us are much good at reading sign. We're farmers, not hunters or scouts or the like."

"We could give it a try," Lou volunteered. "Or, rather, my fiancé could. He's one of the best trackers alive." Perhaps she exaggerated a tad, but only because he was the love of her life.

Jensen's head rose an inch. "Did I just hear you correctly? You're engaged to a 'breed?"

Everyone ignored him, but Zach's blood boiled in his veins. He was making a special effort to control his temper, but there were only so many insults he would abide.

It took a supreme force of will for him to pay attention to what Orville was saying.

"—can certainly use your help, friend. Susie is only five years old. She won't last long on her own. We did find a few bent blades of grass leading to the south, so all our search parties have been scouring the prairie for hours now, with no luck."

"Take me to your camp," Zach said. "I'll do what I can."

Jensen, predictably, objected. "Hold on, Orville. I think you're making a mistake. We can manage on our own."

"No, we can't," Orville countered, "or we'd have found her by now. It's been over three hours." He paused. "Baxter and you can go on looking. I'll escort these two back. Remember, if you spot Susie, fire three shots into the air."

"I think I should go with you," Jensen said.

Orville gave an impatient wave of his hand. "No. You'll do as I say. Or have you forgotten that *I* was elected leader, and not you?"

Jensen's dark eyes blazed spite. "No, I haven't forgotten. But I'm confident everyone will come to their senses once their folly sinks in. In the meantime"—he jerked on his reins—"I'll go along with your wishes." With a last bitter glare at Zach, he trotted off, young Baxter at his heels.

"I'm sorry about how he treated you, mister," Orville said when the pair were out of earshot. "Don't take it personal. He's just a hothead."

Zach said nothing, but he took Jensen's comment very personally. It would be ridiculous to do otherwise. For the moment, though, he let it drop. "We'd better hurry," he suggested. Three hours was a long time for a little girl to be wandering the plains all alone. Predators abounded, as did other dangers equally deadly.

"Certainly. Please, follow me." Orville kneed his sorrel toward the rising smoke. "I'm afraid I've been neglecting my manners. Allow me to introduce myself. Orville Steinmuller, at your service. As Baxter mentioned, there are twelve families in our party. Or twelve couples, I should say. Some have kids, some don't. All told, there are fifty-two in our train."

"And twenty-eight are children?" Lou said in mild surprise. It seemed like an awful lot to her, but then, she guessed that larger wagon trains included even more.

"Yes, ma'am," Orville said. "We're all looking to make a new start for ourselves. To set up our own little community. Originally, we were only going to let couples with children sign up. But at the last minute a couple of Jensen's cousins wanted to come along, and even though they don't have kids, we decided the extra rifles might come in handy."

"Who's acting as your guide?" Zach inquired. Every wagon train relied on an experienced scout or mountaineer to see them safely to the Pacific. Some oldsters, like Jim Bridger and Joseph Walker, were making a fair living at it nowadays.

"We don't have one."

Zach's estimation of the group fell several more notches. As his pa's good friend, Shakespeare McNair, had long maintained, the wilderness was no place for greenhorns and amateurs. "You're taking a terrible risk."

Orville didn't act the least bit concerned. "I'd agree if we were bound for, say, Oregon or California. But we're not. We're heading for the Rockies."

Zach wasn't sure he understood. "You mean, to cross them? In that case, your best bet is South Pass."

"No. We're not going over the Divide. We're looking to settle there."

"*In* the mountains?" Zach couldn't hide his shock. It was practically unheard of. Only four families had already done so: the McNairs, the Clarks, the Kendalls, and the Kings. They had the entire central Front Range pretty much to themselves. In fact, they were the only homesteaders between Pike's Peak and the Canadian border. And Zach liked it that way.

"Why do you sound so shocked?" Orville Steinmuller responded. "We've heard tell there are dozens of lush valleys with fertile soil up there, watered year round. Gardens of Eden, ripe for the taking. Well, we aim to stake a claim to one."

They were nearing the encampment. The twelve wagons were strung out in single file, parked where they had stopped for the night. The stock, Zach observed, had been left to graze, the horses individually hobbled. Only two men were in evidence. Most, he reckoned, were out hunting the little girl.

Lou was suddenly conscious of her appearance. The women and girls all wore pretty dresses, many with bonnets and bows. In her buckskins, with her windblown hair and no cosmetics, she must have presented the perfect picture of plainness. She squared her shoulders and paid no heed to the many quizzical scrutinies directed her way.

The two husky farmers, attended by a group of matronly females, hustled over to meet them.

"What's going on?" a bushy-bearded man demanded. "Who are these newcomers, Brother Steinmuller? Where did they come from?"

Orville halted and jabbed a thumb at the speaker. "This is Jonathan Mathews. He's a Quaker, so he goes around calling everyone 'brother' and 'sister.' " Orville looked at Zach and Lou. "Say, you never did tell me who you folks are."

Zach made the introductions. He was pleased to note that none of those present displayed any of the inexcusable hatred shown by Jensen. Dismounting, he became aware of timid children peeking at Lou and him from behind the security of their parents.

Lou grinned at a girl of six or seven who had the loveliest golden curls. The dozens of sprites brought to mind the talk she'd had with Zach the night before about how many kids they wanted to have. He favored nine or ten. She was partial to three. It was one of the few points on which they couldn't agree.

Orville was explaining how he had met them, and he concluded with "Let's pray Mr. King can be of help. Poor Molly can't take the strain much longer." He rose onto his toes to survey the wagons. "Where is my daughter, anyhow?"

As if on cue, an attractive brunette with an infant in her arms bustled into view and hurried toward them. She wore a green dress with a matching bonnet, and was gnawing on her lower lip as if it were a sapling and she were a beaver. "Pa? Any sign of Susie yet? Tell me you've found her. Please!"

"Not yet, I'm afraid," Orville said. "But there's hope. I found us a man who can track real good."

Molly Mills's eyes were moist as she smiled at Lou and Zach. "I'm eternally grateful for you lending a hand. It's all my fault Susie is missing."

"It is not," Orville said rather harshly. "Quit blaming yourself. How were you to know she'd go traipsing off by her lonesome?"

"I should have heard Susie climb out of the wagon," Molly said, a tear forming. "I should have been more attentive."

"You were sound asleep," Orville said. "You'd been up half the night with the baby and were plumb exhausted."

Lou expected the women to commence bawling at any second. "Show us where your wagon is," she said in the hope it would distract Molly from her grief.

Virtually every last member of the wagon train was now on hand, and they all trailed along as Zach and Lou were led down the line. Some of the children pointed at Zach and giggled and were hushed by their mothers.

The Conestoga in question sat in the shade of an overspreading oak. The grass around it was severely trampled, and at first glance Zach thought he might be dooming the pilgrims to disappointment.

"We found the bent blades there," Orville said, indicating a particular spot ten feet to the south.

Zach cradled the Hawken in the crook of his left elbow and hunkered. The soil was soft enough to bear telltale impressions, but a child of five didn't weigh enough to leave much in the way of tracks. He did spy a heel print close to the rear wheel that was the right size. Moving along the side of the wagon, he discovered another near the water barrel. "Did your daughter help herself to a dipper of water last evening?" he asked.

Molly Mills was astounded. "Yes, as a matter of fact, she did. How on earth did you know?"

Zach returned to the rear. Clods of earth showed where riders had spread outward earlier, churning the dirt and destroying what little sign there might have been. He stared off across the gently waving sea of grass. To the southwest two of the search parties were visible, crisscrossing back and forth. "You say that you first noticed she was missing at sunup?"

"My husband did, yes," Molly answered.

"When they couldn't find her, we turned out the camp," Orville elaborated. "We hollered and hollered, but she never answered."

Zach squatted again, his eyes at about the height a five-year-old's would be. To the south was nothing but grass and more grass. To the north, however, off through the trees, he glimpsed the sparkling surface of the sluggish Platte. Acting on a hunch, he entered the strip of woodland. A few yards in was another heel print. Farther on, etched in a patch of bare earth, was a complete track. Based on the depth, he commented, "You daughter weighs about thirty pounds, I take it?"

A solid wall of curious onlookers had formed a semicircle, intently glued to everything he did. Molly was in the center, hope gleaming where none had been before. "Yes! Thirty-two pounds exactly, last we weighed her."

Orville was scanning the vegetation. "Am I to take it that Susie came this way, and not off across the prairie as we supposed?"

Zach, nodding, drew their attention to another partial print next to a patch of wildflowers. "She broke off a flower and smelled it." A broken stem told him as much. "After looking up at the sky a bit, she moved on."

"You're pulling our legs, mister," a man in shabby overalls said. "There's no way in Hades you can tell all that."

Bending, Zach touched the heel print. "See how the back edge of her shoe angles down instead of lying flat? She saw something overhead—a bird, maybe. Or a squirrel in a tree."

"Well, I'll be!" the skeptic exclaimed.

Louisa was tickled by their awe. The pilgrims were behaving exactly as she had when she first witnessed the tracking ability of her intended. Later, she had been dumbfounded to learn that Zach's father, Nate, was even more skilled. So much so, it was spooky how they read sign with the same ease most people read a book.

The tracks led Zach on a meandering course toward the river. Little Molly had stopped at a tree stump and set the flower on it, then climbed over a low log. She had skipped along for a while, thoroughly enjoying herself, until a thicket forced her to bear wide to the left. "She snagged her dress on a thorn," Zach said, and pried a tiny piece of coppery cloth from a branch to prove it. "There's no blood, so I doubt she pricked herself," he added when the mother clutched her bosom.

To the right were cottonwoods, to the left high weeds, and between the two a gravel bar jutted into the Platte.

"Oh, Lord!" Molly said. "I hope to God she didn't fall in and drown!"

Zach doubted it. As rivers went, the Platte was rather puny. Shallow and slow, it was no more than a glorified stream. There were long stretches where the depth never exceeded six inches. And besides, the child's tracks didn't point toward the waterway. He moved to the high weeds. "I don't think she did."

"If a wild beast got her, I'll never forgive myself," Molly said fearfully. "I tried to warn her, tried to impress on her there are things out here that will eat us, but it wouldn't sink in. She was always so trusting of everyone and everything."

Putting a finger to his lips, Zach parted the outer fringe. He had a fair inkling of what he would find, and there she was, curled into a ball with her thumb stuck in her mouth, deep asleep, so dainty and angelic he thought it was a shame to disturb her. Motioning for quiet, he beckoned to the mother and Orville.

Molly Mills took one look and screeched like a panther. Shoving the infant into her father's arms, she bounded forward.

Poor Susie came up off the ground as if by a cannon. Terror-struck, she blinked in fright and confusion. On seeing Zach, she let out with a screech of her own.

"Susie! Oh, my sweet Susie!" Molly scooped her offspring into her arms and squeezed the girl tight. "I was afraid you were a goner!"

"Ma?" The child squirmed, then saw all the other people and stiffened in bewilderment. "Ma? Why are you crying?"

Zach stepped aside as women rushed up to embrace mother and daughter, and vent their relief. He intended to grab Lou and slip away unnoticed, but it wasn't meant to be. Orville Steinmuller and the other two men came over to congratulate him, each anxious to shake his hand or clap him on the shoulder.

Lou watched it all in hearty amusement. Her betrothed was never entirely at ease around whites, especially large crowds. The years of prejudice and abuse he had suffered were partly to blame. The rest had to do with his retiring nature. In that, Zach was a chip off the old block.

Nate King was as friendly as could be, but given his druthers, he'd rather live off in the wilds than in a village or town. It wasn't that he didn't like people. He could get by on his own, was all, and had no need to rely on anyone else.

Orville was levering Zach's arm as if it were the pump to a well. "You did right fine, friend! Why, you're a regular Daniel Boone or Jim Bridger! Where'd you learn to track like that, anyhow?"

"From my pa and some Shoshones," Zach revealed, while inwardly hankering to get the blazes out of there. The fuss they were raising over so simple a feat embarrassed him.

"They taught you well, Brother King," Jonathan Mathews remarked. "There isn't a man among us who could have done what you did."

Zach shrugged. "All it takes is practice." He tried to shoulder through, but now some women had joined them, eager to relay their gratitude. He glanced at Louisa, who grinned at him as if it were a big joke.

"Where are you bound, Mr. King, if you don't mind my nosiness?" Orville Steinmuller asked.

"The Rockies, same as you."

The older man's eyes lit up like twin candles. "In that case, how about if we treat you and your lady to some coffee and biscuits? I have a proposition I'd like to make, and I'd be obliged if you would hear me out."

It didn't take a genius to deduce what it was. Zach sought to ease them down gently by saying, "We'd like to, we really would, but we have to be on our way. We have a lot of ground to cover before sundown."

Orville's grip was uncommonly strong for a man his age. "Please. Ten minutes of your time is all I'm asking."

"We can't," Zach insisted, and reached for Louisa. The sooner they were out of there, the happier he would be. Her slender fingers enfolded his, and he pivoted to depart. Mathews and several women parted to let him by. But before he had taken two steps, the air was shattered by the blast of gunfire. It came from the vicinity of the covered wagons.

Chapter Two

A general rush ensued toward the wagons, but a bellow from Orville Steinmuller stopped everyone in their tracks. "Women and children, stay here!" he commanded, thrusting the infant into the arms of a gray-haired matriarch. "It could be trouble!" The men hastened on, shoulder to shoulder, their rifles at the ready.

Zach King was losing count of the mistakes the settlers had made. Their first had been having the wagons strung out instead of in a circle for mutual protection. Another had to do with letting their hobbled horses graze at will; the animals should be tied in a string to make it harder for hostiles to steal them. And now here was another. Instead of bunching up and making perfect targets of themselves, the farmers should fan out and stay low, using the brush to its best advantage.

Sighing, Zach followed.

Louisa stayed close to her intended. When she saw how scared some of the women and children were, she almost stayed behind to protect them. But she couldn't. Not when Zach might need her more.

The shooting had stopped. Someone—a man—began shouting. "Where is everyone? Come see what I've found! Steinmuller! Wes! Todd! Where in the world are all of you?"

Zach's grip on the Hawken tightened. The voice was familiar.

Three sweaty horses stood with their heads hung low. Two of the mounts bore saddles, but the third had only a rope bridle. The owner of the third horse was on his knees, his wrists bound behind his back. Over him towered Jensen, who was doing all the yelling. Young Baxter stood nearby, nervously shifting his weight from one booted foot to the other.

At sight of Orville and the other men, Jensen puffed out his chest and crowed, "There you are! Look at what I found skulking about! I bet this filthy heathen knows what happened to your granddaughter, Steinmuller."

Orville, aghast, gawked at the captive. "My Lord. What have you done? What are all those welts and bruises?"

"The uppity heathen wouldn't do as I told him," Jensen said, "so I used some persuasion." He cackled at his wit.

Zach and Lou stepped to one side for a better view. Zach was familiar with most of the tribes between the Rockies and the Mississippi and recognized which one the middled-aged man was from.

Naked from the waist up except for a metal armlet and a beaded necklace, the warrior wore a wool loincloth adorned with beads and a pair of knee-high leggings. An empty sheath hung on his left hip. Other than a stiff quill that ran down the center of his head from his brow to the nape of his neck, his hair had been mostly shaved off. He had finely chiseled, handsome features marred by repeated blows to the face, neck, and shoulders.

"We've found my granddaughter," Orville said.

"What?" Jensen jerked as if slapped.

"She was asleep by the river," Orville detailed, and gestured at the captive. "You had no call to do what you've done. Now we're liable to have his whole tribe down on our heads."

Jensen wasn't willing to admit he had made a grave mistake. "How was I to know you'd found her? When I saw this savage spying on us, I assumed he must have something to do with it."

Zach moved closer. "He's a Pawnee. He was probably curious why so many white men were scouring the prairie. His village can't be far off." Zach based that assumption on the fact that the warrior was so lightly armed.

"Are Pawnees friendly?" Orville asked.

"That depends," Zach answered. By and large, they were. But there had been a few reports of Pawnee atrocities committed against whites found wandering alone or in small parties. And there were other, more sinister accounts, of sacrifices regularly made to the Morning Star, living sacrifices who had their beating hearts carved from their bodies. Zach's pa had a run-in with the Pawnees once, and confirmed the practice still existed.

"Depends on what?" Jonathan Mathews, the Quaker, said.

"Pawnees live in scattered villages," Zach explained. "Each has its own leaders and follows its own council. Some are friendlier to whites than others."

"Do you speak their language?" Orville asked. "Can you talk to this fellow and tell him there's been a terrible misunderstanding, that we mean his people no harm?"

"I don't speak Pawnee," Zach said. But he was fluent in sign, the nigh-universal system of hand symbols used by many of the plains and mountain tribes. Hunkering, he leaned the Hawken on his shoulder to free both hands and signed, "Question. You know finger talk?"

The Pawnee offered no response.

"I called Stalking Coyote," Zach signed, referring to

his Shoshone name. "I friend." Which wasn't entirely true. He had no special fondness for the Pawness, not after his pa's ordeal. But he would do what he could to save the farmers, in spite of themselves.

The Pawnee cocked his head to coldly regard Jensen, then slowly studied everyone else. His contempt for his captors was evident.

Zach tried one more time. "I cut rope. Whites no enemy. Make mistake."

"Big mistake," the Pawnee said in clipped English. "My people not like. They be very angry. Maybe so go on war path."

Flabbergasted, several of the settlers jabbered at once.

"Listen to him!"

"He knows how to talk!"

"What's that about war?"

Zach hushed them with a slash of his arm. "How is it you know the white man's tongue?" he probed.

It was half a minute before the Pawnee deigned to reply. "Many winters past I travel lodge of Great White Father. With Buffalo Hump."

"I've heard that name before, a coon's age ago," Orville said, and suddenly snapped his fingers. "It was in all the newspapers! How that Hump fellow and a bunch of other Indians visited the President."

The Pawnee grunted. "I saw White Father. He give me peace medal."

"You've met the President?" one of the farmers said in disbelief. "Why, even I haven't ever done that."

Hoofbeats heralded the arrival of the rest of the searchers, who had heard the shots. They started throwing questions, one after another. It fell on Orville to fill them in.

Zach placed his hand on his Bowie and had the big knife halfway out when Jensen swiveled toward him.

"What do you think you're doing, mister?"

"Setting him free."

"Like hell you are. You heard the buck. If he goes

back to his people, they're liable to rise up against us. We'd all be wiped out. Leave him be."

Zach wasn't inclined to do any such thing. He bent toward the Pawnee and heard Lou yell in warning. In pure reflex he wrenched aside as the stock of Jensen's rifle swished by his ear. Had it connected, it would have split his skull like an overripe squash. Rotating on the balls of his feet, Zach flung himself upward, reversing his grip on the Bowie as he rose so that when he swung, it was the hilt and not the glistening blade that caught Jensen on the temple with enough force to stagger him.

"Here! Here! What's the meaning of this?" Orville Steinmuller shouted. "Cut that out, both of you!"

Jensen didn't listen. Setting himself, he growled like a wolf at bay and whipped his rifle in a vicious arc. Zach ducked under it, then struck the troublemaker three times in swift succession, battering blows to the chin that rocked Jensen on his heels and ultimately spilled him in the grass with blood trickling from his lower lip.

Dazed but furious, Jensen tried to rise. He froze when the muzzle of a Hawken was shoved into his face.

"If you so much as twitch, I'll blow your brains out," Lou stated matter-of-factly. Ordinarily, she would let Zach settle his own disputes. But some of the farmers appeared ready to intervene, and she couldn't be sure whose side they would take.

"Why, you little hussy," Jensen growled, rising just a bit more.

Lou thumbed back the hammer. The metallic click froze him in place, and doubt mixed with a tinge of fear replaced the anger in his eyes.

"Careful, girl! Don't do anything you'll regret."

"I wouldn't regret it one bit," Lou said sweetly. And she meant it. She had taken human lives before, always when her own or someone dear to her was threatened, always when she had no other option. But she had taken them, nonetheless, and she wouldn't hesitate to do so again. She would think no more of snuffing out Jensen than she would of snuffing out a candle. Or, even more apt, of crushing a loathsome bug.

Jensen seemed to realize as much. "Take up with a heathen and you take up heathen ways. Is that it?" he blustered. But he didn't attempt to gain his feet.

Zach was annoyed at Louisa for butting in. Jensen deserved to be beaten within an inch of his life, or maybe to have an ear cut off. It might teach him a lesson. Then again, Zach pegged the hothead as the type who was incapable of learning to respect others. Bending, he cut the rope that bound the Pawnee. "Off you go."

The warrior, rubbing his wrists, slowly rose. "I thank you, Stalking Coyote." In sign, he added, "Leave whites. They bad medicine." Without further ado, he wheeled, vaulted onto his pinto, and jabbed his heels against its sides. Head high, his back ramrod straight, he rode off to the southeast.

"Someone stop him!" Jensen fumed. "Wes! Todd! Baxter! Shoot the bastard, or he'll bring his whole tribe down on us!"

"No!" Orville exclaimed. "We're not murderers! All we can do is trust in Providence to see us through."

"Amen to that, Brother Steinmuller," Jonathan Mathews said.

Zach strode to the bay and raised a moccasin to the stirrup. The Pawnee had a point. As inept as the whites were, it was only a matter of time before disaster befell them. He hoisted himself up.

"Wait! Please!" Orville scooted over. "Stay awhile. At least until you hear my proposition."

"I know what it is, and I'm not interested," Zach said.

"At least sleep on it," Orville said. "We'll treat you to supper, and you can give us your answer in the morning." He placed a hand on Zach's leg. "We need someone like you, someone who knows the lay of the land and how to deal with Indians and such. Guide us to the mountains and we'll make it worth your while. Between the twelve families, we should be able to rustle up over a hundred dollars as payment."

"Are you crazy?" one of the new arrivals interjected. "That's about all the money we can spare."

"It's worth every cent if it means we reach the Rockies safely," Orville argued.

"Being paid isn't important," Zach said. "I just don't want to do it." He could think of few less appealing chores than nursemaiding over fifty blockheads for days on end.

Steinmuller didn't know how to take no for an answer. "Think of the women and children! Without your help, some of them might not make it."

"You should have thought of that before leaving Ohio," Zach said. Better yet, they should never have *left* Ohio.

"I'm begging you, son," Orville said. "What's happened today has taught me the error of our ways. You're our salvation. The Almighty sent you to us to be our guardian angel."

Zach remembered artists' renderings of angels in his father's Bible. Twisting, he made a show of examining his shoulder blades. "Strange. I don't see any wings."

"Please don't—" Orville began.

"I'm sorry." Zach reined westward.

Lou had forked leather, but she hesitated. They should at least hear the settlers out, she thought.

"Are you coming?" Zach asked over a shoulder.

"Good luck, Mr. Steinmuller," Lou told the oldster, and clucked to the mare.

Neither of them said anything for the better part of an hour. Zach didn't look back once, although Lou did, repeatedly. The last time, a tiny figure in a dress was by the last wagon, waving farewell.

Noon found them in a glade beside the bubbling Platte. Zach watered the horses while Louisa perched on a boulder and ran a hand through her hair.

"I've been thinking . . ."

"I don't want to hear it," Zach said testily.

"Is that so? But you're going to, whether you want to or not." Lou persisted. "Those people don't stand a prayer on their own, and we both know it. Since we're bound for the same stretch of mountains they are, why not hook up with them? What would it hurt?"

"You're forgetting Jensen."

"One bad apple spoils the whole barrel? Is that what you're telling me? What about the children? Twenty-eight of them, weren't there? And one a baby."

"We're not obliged to help a bunch of strangers."

"Aren't we?"

Zach wondered if she fully appreciated what she was asking him to do. The Rockies were at least five hundred miles distant. Maybe more like six hundred. At the rate heavy wagons traveled, twelve to fifteen miles a day, on average, it would take five weeks, minimum, to make the journey.

"What has you so spooked?" Louisa asked.

"We won't get home until the leaves start to turn."

"So we're delayed a couple of weeks? Your folks won't mind. No, there has to be more to it than that. I know you too well, Stalking Coyote." Rising, Lou walked over and looped her arm in his. "What's really eating you?"

Zach couldn't rightly say. Conflicting emotions tore at his insides, creating a whirlpool of indecision. On the one hand, he readily admitted the settlers needed help. On the other, he might be biting off more than he could chew, as the old saw went. He'd be responsible for fifty-two lives, the majority women and children. One wrong decision, a single lapse in judgment, could spell doom for them all.

Lou pressed her cheek to his chest. She had always felt a special closeness to Zach, a sense that the two of them were somehow linked in more than mind and heart. Soul mates, was how she liked to describe it. And she flattered herself that because of their special bond, she was especially sensitive to his thoughts and moods. Now she pecked him on the jaw and commented, "I recollect your pa telling me that he's led a wagon train or two west in his time."

Zach nodded. "Once we we went all the way to the Pacific. I'd never seen the ocean before, and I spent days playing in the sand and surf."

"Then I ask you, if your pa can do it, why not you?"

"In case you haven't noticed, I'm not half the man he is."

Lou embraced Zach, brazenly kissing him full on the mouth. "You're trying to convince the wrong person. As far as I'm concerned, anything your pa can do, you can do, too." She kissed him again. "My ma used to say we can't go through life judging our peck by someone else's bushel."

"You really want me to do this, don't you?"

"It's not so much what I want as what we *have* to do," Lou corrected him. "We'll never be able to live with ourselves if we let those folks blunder their way to oblivion."

Now it was Zach's turn to kiss her. For all the jokes men told about how scatterbrained women were, the truth was that women could be just as logical as the males of the species, if not more so. "All right. We'll wait here for them to catch up and give Steinmuller the good news."

The next several hours were idyllic. They took off their moccasins to wade in the Platte, splashing water on one another and frolicking like a pair of ten-year-olds. They ate some of the jerked venison they had stocked up on at a trading post on the outskirts of St. Louis. They lay in the sun, as content as it was possible for two people to be. Then, along about four o'clock, Louisa stirred and marked the position of the sun.

"They should have been here by now."

"We'll give them another hour." Zach didn't want to

budge. Precious moments such as these were too few and far between to be wasted.

"Maybe something happened. Maybe the Pawnees paid them a visit."

"Too soon." Zach was too comfortable to contemplate moving. "The Pawnees aren't likely to show until tomorrow morning, if at all."

"We should go check anyway."

Cracking an eyelid, Zach savored the sight of her lovely upturned face. To him, she was the prettiest girl alive. The blue in her eyes was bluer than the sea, the red in her lips redder than cherries. He had never expected to see the day where he would give his heart to another, yet she had claimed it as if it were her natural right to do so, and never once had he had any qualms or reservations. Love, he reckoned, was peculiar that way.

"Well?" Louisa goaded.

Five minutes later, they were in the saddle and retracing their steps eastward. In the trees a robin warbled. Closer, in a dense patch of brush, sparrows flitted. High overhead a red hawk soared, its long wings outstretched.

"I miss your folks, you know," Lou mentioned. She had been thinking of Nate and Winona King a lot of late. Soon they would be her father-in-law and mother-in-law, the only father and mother she had since her own had passed onto their reward. Being a full-fledged part of their family would be wonderful.

"Makes two of us," Zach said. He even missed his sister, although he'd never in a million years admit as much. Evelyn was the biggest pain since toothaches were invented. She never tired of teasing and tricking him and generally doing all in her power to make his life miserable.

"After we're officially man and wife," Lou broached a subject she had been pondering of late, "do you think the Shoshones will want to adopt me into their tribe?"

"I honestly can't say," Zach replied. The tribe had

adopted his pa and Evelyn and him, but that was because his mother was Shoshone. Whether they would see fit to do the same with his new wife remained to be seen.

Lou was considering another issue sparked by her query. How "official" would their union be? Whom could they get to perform the rites? Zach would be perfectly content with a Shoshone ceremony, but she preferred to be married by a minister, if at all possible. Not that she was a stickler for legality, or that she felt Indian customs were somehow inferior or anything like that. But since she was old enough to remember, she had dreamed of one day standing before a man of the cloth and reciting the vow that would bind her to the love of her life for eternity.

"Listen," Zach abruptly said, reining up.

Lou had been so deep in thought, she hadn't heard the faint pop of rifles and pistols. "The settlers! They're under attack!"

"Too soon," Zach quoted his previous opinion, and swore under his breath at his own stupidity. "Let's light a shuck."

Together they broke into a gallop, speeding parallel with the trees, the manes and tails of their horses flying. Zach's bay was capable of outdistancing Lou's mare, but he was unwilling to leave her behind.

The *crack-crack-crack* of the guns grew steadily louder.

Zach wanted to kick himself for miscalculating. He'd taken it for granted the Pawnees would hold council before paying the whites a visit, a council bound to last well into the wee hours of the night. That was what the Shoshones would do. But apparently the Pawnees were short on talk and long on action.

When they were near enough to hear strident war whoops, Zach veered to the left, into the undergrowth, and slowed to a cautious walk. Another hundred yards brought them within sight of the conflict.

"Land sakes!" Lou declared.

Forty or fifty warriors were taking part in the raid. Some were armed with bows, some with lances, some with war clubs. Only a few had rifles. In constant motion, yipping like frenzied coyotes, they swooped down on the Conestogas.

Lou hefted her Hawken. "Those pilgrims don't stand a chance!"

At first glance, it sure seemed that way. But Zach noticed that none of the Pawnees were firing arrows or their rifles as they raced along the row of wagons. Most were content to swing onto the off side of their war horses, rising up after they had gone down the entire row to whoop in delight. A few, more courageous than their companions, darted in near enough to strike a white with the butt of a lance or club. Then they, too, would dash off, howling and laughing.

"Wait a minute," Lou said. "Something isn't quite right."

"The Pawnees aren't out for blood," Zach said. He didn't see a single body. And in light of how long the clash had lasted, there should be plenty. It was fortunate the farmers couldn't hit the broad side of a barn at twenty paces.

"Why not?"

"The Pawnees are giving the whites a taste of their own medicine, paying them back for what Jensen did," Zach speculated.

"Then all we have to do is sit here until the Pawnees tire of their game and leave," Lou said happily.

It wasn't quite that simple, Zach reflected. At the moment the Pawnees were content to pretend counting coup. But should the farmers shoot one, the warriors would attack in earnest, overwhelming the vastly outnumbered whites with ease. "We have to get Orville's people to lower their guns," he said.

"How's that?" Lou responded. As long as the Pawnees weren't really on the war path, she didn't understand why they should tempt fate.

A burly warrior wielding a lance raced in close to the wagons at the far end and flew along the row as if his mount had wings on its hoofs. He ducked onto the far side, his forearm hooked over the animal's neck, a split second before one of the farmers' guns belched lead and smoke.

"Wait here until I signal you," Zach said, kneeing the bay toward the open.

"Not on your life," Lou informed him. Where he went, she went, and he had better get used to the idea.

There was no time for debate. Zach saw Tommy Baxter move into the path of the onrushing warrior. "Damn!" He exploded from cover, streaking past a Pawnee.

Baxter planted himself, wedged his long gun to his right shoulder, and took deliberate aim.

"Baxter! Don't!" Zach yelled, waving his rifle over head. But the young farmer's back was to him, and the din drowned out his warning.

Lou glued the mare to the bay's flank, prepared to protect her beloved's life with her own if need be. She saw some of the farmers pointing, saw some of the Pawnees doing likewise.

Zach rose in the stirrups. *"Baxter! Don't shoot!"*

The burly Pawnee was almost on top of him. The warrior had his face pressed to the side of his war horse and didn't catch sight of Baxter until almost the last possible moment. Then, heaving upright, the Pawnee hauled on the reins, seeking to avoid a collision and spare the settler from being trampled into the dirt.

Just then, Tommy Baxter fired.

Chapter Three

Zach King had tried his best. Still thirty feet from the young farmer, all he could do was watch in helpless frustration as a lead ball slammed into the burly Pawnee's shoulder and sent the warrior toppling. Tommy Baxter tried to leap out of the path of the war horse, but he wasn't quite fast enough. Its shoulder caught him in the chest, bowling him over.

Zach dismounted on the fly, nearly pitching onto his face when he stumbled. Righting himself, he ran to the fallen Pawnee and sank onto a knee.

The warrior was on his back, an acorn-sized hole oozing blood high in his shoulder. His eyes were open, but he was in shock and didn't react when Zach bent low to examine him. Carefully raising the man's shoulder, Zach found the exit wound, a nasty cavity rimmed by ragged flesh and pouring scarlet.

"How is he?" Lou had brought the mare to a stop right beside them, but she stayed in the saddle to be better able to protect Zach or get him out of there should the need arise. Many of the Pawnees had witnessed the incident and were swiftly streaming toward their fallen companion.

"He's hurt bad," Zach said. The ball, though, had missed the man's vital organs, so with prompt medical attention the odds of recovery were excellent.

Baxter ran up, limping slightly. "I got him!" he proudly beamed. "Did you see? I finally brought one of them down!"

"And maybe killed your family and everyone else in the bargain!" Zach said gruffly. "Get back to your wagon! Hurry!"

"What are you talking about?" Baxter said, confused. "What did I do wrong?"

"I'll explain later," Zach said, and gave the young farmer a shove. Some of the Pawnees were near enough to turn Baxter into a porcupine with their arrows and lances. But none fired. Baxter, bewildered, shuffled toward his wagon, moving faster once he saw the converging warriors.

The wounded Pawnee grimaced, then galvanized to life. He tried to rise, wincing in agony, and was about to push Zach away when his eyes narrowed and he blurted what seemed to be a question in the Pawnee tongue.

Zach imagined the warrior was puzzled because he wasn't white. Rather than let go to use sign, Zach helped the man to sit up. By then hoofs were drumming like thunder in his ears and Pawnees were vaulting from their mounts. One practically threw Zach to one side, but Zach didn't take offense. He would do the same if it were a friend of his.

Lou was an anxious wreck. Seven, eight, ten warriors had gathered, with the remainder on their way. At any moment any one of them might turn on Zach. Catching his eye, she motioned for him to get out of there, but he gave a toss of his head. Lou could only pray he knew what he was doing.

The farmers, Zach was grateful to see, had stopped

firing, largely thanks to Orville Steinmuller, who was bellowing for them to do just that.

More Pawnees arrived. Among them was the one Zach was waiting for, the middle-aged warrior Jensen had captured, the warrior who spoke a smattering of English. He appeared to be a man of some importance, for when he hopped from his horse the others stepped out of his way.

The wounded one had been hoisted to his feet but was so weak he couldn't stand unaided. He sagged as the middle-aged warrior examined him.

Other Pawnees were casting dire looks at the settlers. Zach felt it prudent to comment, "The whites thought it was for real. They didn't know you weren't trying to kill them."

The middle-aged warrior turned. "We touch them. We ride off. They see that with own eyes."

"But they didn't know what it meant," Zach said. The Pawnees had been putting on a display of courage and horsemanship to demonstrate their prowess and put the farmers in their place, to show that white men couldn't go around beating Pawnees with impunity.

The warrior glanced at the wagons. "Maybeso you speak true. Whites do not think as the Skidi think."

"If they think at all," Zach quipped. He found it highly ironic that he, of all people, was defending those who routinely treated him as if he were a vile maggot.

The corners of the warrior's mouth quirked upward. "One day I, Eagle Feather, chief of the Skidi, go to the other side. I will ask spirit father, Tirawa, why he make whites. Maybeso Tirawa drunk on firewater."

Zach grinned, then got right to the crux of the problem Baxter had unwittingly caused. "Does this end it? Or will you want blood?"

Eagle Feather slipped an arm around the wounded warrior to help get him on a horse. "We go. Buffalo Hump live, this end. Buffalo Hump die, the grass run red with white blood."

The Pawnees gathered up their horses and trotted off. Judging by their countenances, some wanted to tear into the settlers then and there, but they did as their leader desired.

No sooner had the warriors dwindled in the distance than the farmers poured from their wagons to congratulate Zach.

Orville Steinmuller was at the forefront. "Well met, friend! I didn't quite hear what you told those fellows, but you've saved us. We owe you our lives."

Others clapped Zach on the back and told him what a fine job he had done. When one remarked, "You prevented a massacre! We're forever in your debt!", it was the proverbial last straw.

Zach couldn't keep quiet any longer. Shrugging a hand off his shoulder, he raised his voice so they'd all hear what he had to say. "You're not out of the woods yet. If that warrior dies, the rest will be back." He made sure he had their undivided attention, then continued. "If that happens, you'll have no one to blame but yourselves. Those Pawnees weren't out for your scalps."

"Are you insane?" a farmer said. "They swooped down on us like a swarm of riled bees."

"Did they kill anyone?" Zach said. "Did they fire their arrows or throw their lances?" He answered his own question before anyone else could. "No. All they did was yell a lot and hit some of you. It's called counting coup. They were showing how brave they are, was all."

Jensen snorted. "How were we supposed to know? What would you have had us do? Stand there like simpletons while they rode down on us?"

The Quaker, Mathews, cleared his throat. "As God is my witness, Brother King, I, too, sincerely thought they were out for blood."

Orville saw a golden opportunity to press his case. "This is another example, Mr. King, of why we need someone like you to guide us to the Rockies. I took it for granted we could do it on our own, but after seeing how you tracked my granddaughter down, and now how you've dealt with the Pawnees, I'm ready to admit I made a mistake. So please, on behalf of us all, I'm asking you to accept the offer I made you."

"Think of the women and children, Brother," Mathews threw in.

Actually, were it not for the women and children, Zach wouldn't even consider accepting. He couldn't let the pigheadedness of their menfolk cost them their lives, not when he was in a position to do something about it. Louisa had been right. "There are conditions," he announced, part of him hoping they would refuse to accept his terms.

"Name them," Orville Steinmuller said.

"If you hire me, I'm in charge. Complete charge. Everyone does what I say, when I say. No exceptions." Zach had learned that from his pa. "I decide how far we travel each day. I choose when and where we'll stop for the night."

Orville smiled. "Sounds reasonable to me."

"But not to me," Frank Jensen said. "I didn't come on this trek to be bossed around by someone half my age."

"Even if they have ten times your experience?" Orville challenged. "I should think our young friend has proven his ability."

"Not to my satisfaction," Jensen declared. "I say we put it to a vote. If we do, you'll find that most agree with me."

"Will you kindly excuse us for about five minutes?" Orville asked Zach. "Before we left Ohio we wrote up an agreement on how things would run. Our charter, we call it. All major decisions are to be decided by a show of hands."

"Go right ahead," Zach said, "but remember, if I take over, no more voting from here on out. I'll have the final say. My word will be law."

Zach had heard his father say the exact same thing

once when the members of a wagon train gave him guff. Pilgrims like these didn't seem to appreciate it was for their own good. Often, decisions vital to their survival had to be made on the spur of the moment. Petty squabbling couldn't be abided.

"Listen to him," Jensen muttered. "He can't wait to crack the whip."

Claiming the bay, Zach walked into the shade. Lou rode beside him, dismounting when he stopped. Almost immediately some of the women and children materialized, among them Molly and Susie Mills. The mother brought a dipper of water, the little girl a handful of jerked venison.

"We thought you might like these," Molly said.

Since Zach made no move to accept, Lou did, saying, "It was awful sweet of you. We haven't had a bite since breakfast."

"Please accept an invite to join us for supper," Molly offered. "It's the least we can do after what you've done for us." She reached for Lou's hand. "Allow me to introduce you to the other ladies. I'm sure they're all dying to make your acquaintance."

Lou glanced at Zach, who had sat down with his back to a tree trunk. She was flattered that he had done the right thing mainly to please her. Lou took it as yet another example of the deep love he bore for her. "I'll only be a moment."

"No hurry," Zach said. He was watching the men.

Lou saw that Steinmuller and Jensen were in a heated argument, Jensen no doubt doing all in his power to sway the other farmers to side with him. As Shakespeare McNair once put it, "Some people are born with so much acid in their systems, they have sour dispositions from cradle to grave."

The introductions were made so fast, Louisa was afraid she'd forget half the names. Of the twelve women, the oldest was Steinmuller's wife, Agatha, who looked to be in her mid to late fifties. Rather late in life, Lou thought, for someone to uproot themselves and go traipsing off to the Rockies.

The only one who didn't shake Lou's hand was Jensen's wife, Charlotte. And that had more to do with how shy Charlotte was than with her being anything like her spouse. She always had her head bowed, as if she were afraid of looking anyone in the eye. She also only spoke when addressed, and then so softly she was hard to understand. Charlotte wore a dress with unusually long sleeves and a high neckline, a garment more fitting for winter than summer, but she didn't seem to mind the heat. On her left temple was a small bruise, which Lou didn't give much attention to.

Another memorable character was Jonathan Mathews's wife, Tamar. She was as big as a she-bear and as outgoing as could be. Her attire consisted of an exceedingly plain homespun dress and a peculiar circular sort of bonnet Lou had never seen before. On being introduced, Tamar gave Lou a huge hug, exclaiming, "It's a grand pleasure to meet you, Sister. If I can ever be of service, you only have to let me know."

Two of the women were rather reserved, almost aloof: Bertha and Verna Lattigore. As Lou understood it, the pair were sisters, married to cousins of Frank Jensen. Neither had children. Both were waspish and stern, gargoyles who looked at Lou as if she were plague-infested and didn't care to be anywhere near her.

Little Susie Mills glued herself to Lou's side. Every time Lou so much as turned, Susie was there, doting on her with admiring eyes. Lou didn't quite grasp why until Molly explained.

"My daughter was scared to death when she wandered off this morning and got lost. I've told her how you and your fiancé saved her life, and she's grateful."

"Zach did it, not me," Lou reminded them.

"Is he an Indian?" Susie inquired.

"Hush, child," Molly instantly scolded. "Questions

like that offend folks. Whether he is or isn't doesn't make no nevermind at all."

"I'm not offended," Lou said, squatting in front of the girl. "Yes, he's part Shoshone. They're a friendly tribe who live in the Rockies."

"You love him?" Susie asked with the bluntness typical of those her tender age.

"Susan W. Mills!" Molly said.

Lou grinned. "Yes, I love him very much."

"Even though he's part Indian?"

"That doesn't make him bad," Lou said.

Susie contemplated the statement. "It doesn't? Then why do some people say bad things about Indians?"

"Indians are just like whites," Lou said. "Some are good, some are mean. But some whites think that makes all Indians mean. Which isn't true."

Verna Lattigore made a sniffing noise. "Easy for you to say, Miss Clark. But we've heard too many tales of too many atrocities to trust any Injun. Or anyone who's part Injun." For emphasis, Verna cast a glance pregnant with meaning at Zach.

Lou had to remind herself she was a lady. Or she was *supposed* to be. Although she sorely wanted to belt the woman in the mouth, she contented herself with replying, "It's easy to cast stones when you think that you're better than the person you're casting them at."

Tamar Mathews laughed, which didn't go over well with the two sisters. As icy as glaciers, they withdrew a few yards to be by themselves.

"Pay them no mind," Tamar said. "They're forever looking at the bad side of things. Frankly, since they think so poorly of this world and everyone in it, the Good Lord would do us all a favor by whisking them down below, where they'd really have something to complain about."

Louisa chuckled. "I thought Quakers always turned the other cheek?"

"That we do, sweet sister," Tamar said, "but we're also called onto minister the truth. And the truth is, those two are always carping about something or another. Cut their skin and you're liable to find scales underneath."

Charlotte Jensen gave everyone pause by saying, "Do you like it up in the mountains, Miss Clark?"

"I couldn't see living anywhere else," Lou answered. Once, though, she'd felt the complete opposite. When her pa first broached the idea of venturing deep into the wilderness after beaver, she'd objected. Back then, the mountains were as alien to her as the moon. She'd wanted nothing to do with them. Then along came Zach, and her attitude did a total turnaround. Lou couldn't quite decide if her change of heart was brought on by her affection for him or whether she had just grown accustomed to life in the high country.

One thing Lou did know. She would never go back east. She could never take to dwelling in a city again. Not after experiencing the freedom and beauty of the Rockies. Not after tasting life as their Maker meant it to be.

It was funny. Lou never used to think much about things like that. She had always taken it for granted she *was* free, that she lived in the best country in the world, where a person could do as they pleased without anyone to say different. But she had been kidding herself.

In the States people were under the yoke of politicians who more often than not passed laws the people despised. Laws that hemmed the people in. Laws that formed the bars of invisible cages few realized were there. Laws politicians claimed were for the good of all but which benefited the few.

In the Rockies no one told anyone else what to do. Or how they should live. Folks could do as they pleased, always bearing in mind that if they stepped out of line, if they stepped on someone's toes, they suffered the consequences. And on occasion the consequences were fatal.

Another woman, Tommy Baxter's young wife, Elizabeth, roused Lou from her reflection.

"You've got more gumption than I do, Miss Clark. It took my husband over a year to convince me to make this journey. I was dead set against it."

"How come?"

"Need you ask? The short and sweet of it is that it's too dangerous. We have no guarantee that even if we find a valley we like and settle there, we'll still be alive a year from now."

"No one knows when their time will come," Lou mentioned. "Why fret over what we can't control?"

"I'm not. But there's a difference between going to a zoo to see a tiger and putting your head in the tiger's mouth."

Lou had to admit she had a point.

Zach was scanning the prairie for sign of the Pawnees when the twelve farmers marched toward him. By the scowl on Jensen, the result of the vote wasn't difficult to guess. Orville Steinmuller announced the decision.

"By a nine-to-three margin, friend, you're now our official guide. We'd be pleased if you started right away."

Who were the three dissenters? Zach wondered. Frank Jensen was a given. The other two, Zach suspected, were Jensen's cousins, Todd and Wes Lattigore. Brothers, they dressed in identical somber black pants and shirts, and, unlike the rest of the men, always wore a pair of flintlocks tucked under their belts. Neither betrayed a glimmer of friendliness. Zach didn't doubt for a second that, given the chance, they'd gladly put a lead ball in his back.

"What do you say?" Orville asked.

"Everyone agreed to my terms?"

"Majority rules, son. Those who were against the idea have to do as the rest of us want, whether they like it or not. We're yours to command."

Frank Jensen's scowl deepened.

"Call everyone together," Zach said, standing. "I'll let them know how it's going to be." The settlers dispersed to obey except for the Lattigore brothers. As flinty as quartz, they minced no bones.

"We don't like you, boy," Todd said. He was the oldest by a few years, somewhere in his late twenties, and built as solidly as a wall.

"That we don't," Wes stressed. He had a large hooked nose that lent him the aspect of a turkey buzzard.

"You'd be doing yourself a favor if you rode on out," Todd said.

"While you still can," Wes amended.

Todd was like a riverboat picking up steam. "We're not taking orders from no half-breed—not now, not ever. You can talk until you're blue in the face and we'll do as we see fit. Raise a fuss and you'll regret it."

"Regret it a lot," Wes parroted.

Todd's jutting jaw bobbed. "That's not all. We expect you to treat our ladyfolk with respect. We've heard tell how you 'breeds are, and we won't tolerate any shenanigans."

"None," Wes echoed.

Zach didn't know whether to laugh or club them over the head. He compromised by remarking, "Thanks for letting me know where you stand. In a few minutes, I'll be doing the same."

The Lattigores, smirking smugly, went to join Frank Jensen.

Quietly simmering, Zach almost changed his mind. Why, he asked himself, should he put his life and that of the woman he loved at risk for people who couldn't care less? Jensen and the cousins would be thorns in his side the entire trip, forever criticizing and carping and waiting for him to make mistakes they could exploit. Why should he subject himself to their needless aggravation? To their mindless prejudice? True, not all whites were like that. Not all whites judged others by the color of their skin. But men like Jensen and the Lattigores had been making his life miserable for as long as he could remember, and Zach would just as well not have to deal with them day in and day out for weeks on end. He was inviting trouble.

The sight of the approaching women and children calmed him. Zach didn't want their deaths on his conscience. And tragedy was bound to result if the men were left to carry on as they had.

Zach wasn't one of those who believed females needed continual looking after, as if they were no more than overgrown girls who couldn't so much as lace up their footwear on their own. His mother, who was as strong-willed and independent a woman as ever lived, had taught him females were every bit as capable as males.

Even so, Zach felt an instinctive urge to protect them. An urge reinforced by his pa, who had impressed on him from the day he was old enough to understand that a man must always be ready and willing to safeguard the fairer gender from any and all threats.

Shoshone warriors were the same. While Shoshone women often helped defend villages and sometimes went on raids, it was the men who bore the greater share of the burden. It became second nature for them to put the welfare of the women and children before their own.

So now, as the whites assembled in a semicircle, Zach decided to stick with his decision. He would see it through, as Lou wanted. As for Jensen and Jensen's cousins, he'd do whatever it took to keep them in line.

A flash of memory brought a smile to Zach's lips. He recollected being with his father about two years earlier and facing a group just like this one. Most of what his father had said was fresh enough in his mind to quote: "I'll make this short. I'm your new guide. From now on I'm in charge. Do as I tell you and we have a good chance of reaching the Rockies. Buck me and you'll bring no end of trouble down on your heads."

"We'll do whatever you want," Orville Steinmuller interrupted. "You can count on our complete cooperation."

To say Zach was skeptical was putting it mildly. He'd as soon believe that buffalo could sprout wings and fly.

Tommy Baxter had a reasonable question. "What is it, exactly, you'll expect of us?"

"Every morning we'll pull out at sunrise," Zach quoted his father. "Not a minute later. Anyone who doesn't have their team hitched and ready to go will be left behind. We'll stop once at midday for about half an hour to rest the animals. Each evening I'll pick where we're to camp. The wagons will be parked in a circle, and the stock will be tethered to a rope. Guards will be posted in shifts so everyone gets some sleep. Those are the basic rules." He paused. "Any questions or complaints?"

Jonathan Mathews raised a hand as if he were a schoolboy seeking permission from a teacher.

"Yes?" Zach spurred when the Quaker didn't say anything.

"What about the Lord's day?"

"What about it?"

"Well, surely we'll take it off? Read Scripture. Six days man is to toil, but on the seventh he must rest. Back in Ohio, I insisted it be part of the charter."

"From this point on, your charter, as you call it, isn't worth the paper it's written on," Zach responded. "And in case you haven't heard, there are no Sundays west of the Mississippi. In order to reach the Rockies before the snows hit, we'll travel seven days a week."

Murmuring broke out.

"That's the way it will be," Zach declared. Whether they liked it or not. "Since this day is already half over, we'll head out at first light. But I want the wagons in a circle, with the stock inside. Get cracking."

The moment of truth had come. Would they do as Zach instructed or give him grief? To his relief, they headed for their respective Conestogas. But Zach wasn't deceived. The wagon train was a powder keg waiting for the right spark to set it off. All he could do was hope he wasn't caught in the explosion.

Chapter Four

Four days later, Zach's premonition came true.

By then the settlers had settled into a routine. Each morning they roused themselves from under their blankets well before first light. The women prepared breakfast while the men hitched the teams. Eggs or pancakes were generally favored, the eggs ingeniously packed in flour to prevent breakage.

As soon as the golden crown of the sun framed the eastern horizon, Zach forked leather and ordered them to head out. Until noon they paralleled the winding Platte, bearing steadily westward. After a brief break, on they plodded. Along about sunset, Zach had them circle the wagons and bed down.

It was slow going, the heavily laden Conestogas moving at a snail's pace. Or so it seemed to Zach, who chafed at their progress and longed to hurry on, to reach the Rockies that much sooner.

Lou didn't mind nearly as much. She liked being around the other women, liked chatting with them and playing with their children. Except for Charlotte Jensen and the Lattigores, they accepted her with friendly, open arms.

When Zach rode point well ahead of the train, as he often did to scout the course of the river and check for sign, the constant swishing of the high grass reminded him of the rhythmic hiss of ocean surf. The shallow waterway and the vegetation rimming it were the only variety in the vast sea of shimmering prairie. There was grass, grass everywhere, for as far as the eye could see.

The Platte itself was a godsend, salvation in liquid form. Without it the pilgrims would soon wither and expire, winding up as so many bleached bones. Being able to quench their thirst and water their stock relieved Zach of a major worry.

Food posed no problem, either, at least for the foreseeable future. Each family had brought plenty of provisions. And along the river there was wildlife in abundance; deer, rabbits, quail, a variety of game animals and birds, all theirs for the taking.

Everything seemed to be working in their favor, but Zach knew all too well that the prairie was fraught with peril. It was a lot like the ocean in that respect, also. On the surface, all appeared serene. Underneath, though, peril perpetually lurked, waiting to claim the lives of the unwary and the foolhardy.

Farmer Jacob Marsh learned the truth the hard way. The third evening out, he walked his team to the Platte to let them drink. Squatting beside a boulder, he bent to dip his hand in, then turned to marble. A huge rattlesnake had reared, its tail vibrating, its thick body coiled, its head held high with its deadly fangs exposed, about to strike.

Zach heard one of the man's horses nicker in fright. Spying the serpent, he snapped the Hawken to his shoulder and fired just as the reptile lunged. The heavy lead ball cored the rattler where its jaw joined its body and the snake fell with a thud, landing outstretched with its drippings fangs an inch from Marsh's foot.

The farmer scrambled back, sweat dotting his brow, as others came on the run.

"It's always best to keep your eyes skinned," Zach advised.

"I didn't think—" Marsh blurted, and gulped.

"No, you didn't," Zach said curtly. "Snakes like to sun themselves on big rocks just like the one next to you."

"I know. But it wasn't on the rock, or I'd have seen it."

"Rattlers do their hunting at night," Zach mentioned, irritated the man would quibble. "Odds were, it had just climbed down to go on the prowl when you blundered by."

"I'll be more careful in the future," Marsh vowed.

"I hope so, for your sake."

Twenty-four hours later, the blowup occurred.

Zach had called a halt in a grassy bend of the river where they were partly screened on three sides by trees and undergrowth. After the teams were tethered and the cook fires crackling, he cradled the Hawken and went in search of Louisa, who had strolled toward the Platte with little Susie Mills and other children.

As Zach rounded a cluster of saplings, he saw three women at the water's edge. It was Charlotte Jensen and her kin, Bertha and Verna Lattigore, filling buckets. An inner voice urged him to avoid them. The Lattigores hated his guts, and Charlotte hadn't said two words to him since he hooked up with the train. But he kept on walking, unwilling to back off, to let their prejudice get the better of him. "Howdy, ladies," he said good-naturedly. "Have you seen Louisa?"

The Lattigores uncoiled, glaring at him as if he were a rabid wolf about to assault them, their disdain thick enough to be sliced with a meat cleaver.

"We don't keep track of your hussy's whereabouts," Bertha snapped.

Charlotte was on one knee, her bucket in the Platte. "I thought I saw your lady friend over yonder," she said, pointing eastward.

"Thank you," Zach said.

Verna Lattigore switched her withering contempt from him to Charlotte. "What's gotten into you? Being civil to a 'breed?"

"Wait until we tell your husband," Bertha said.

Raw fright made Charlotte's mousy features pale. "There's no call for that. All I did was answer Mr. King's question."

"You don't call his kind 'mister,' " Verna said.

Zach would have liked to push both sisters into the river. Smiling at Charlotte, he started to slant in the direction she had indicated. Almost too late, he heard the pounding of onrushing boots, and spun. Todd and Wes Lattigore were nearly on top of him. Both tossed their rifles aside as he began to bring up his own. The next moment, they slammed into him like a pair of enraged bulls.

The impact lifted Zach off his feet. One of the women shouted something as Zach was smashed flat on his back with the two older men on top, their fists flailing madly. He caught a blow on the chin that set pinpoints of dazzling light to flickering like a swarm of fireflies. The Hawken was ripped from his grasp.

"We warned you, 'breed!" Todd declared.

"Yep!" Wes mimicked.

"Now you're going to get what's been coming to you," Todd said.

Wes cocked a fist on high. "What you got coming!"

Pure rage surged through Zach in a fiery flush. From deep within, from the core of his being, erupted an overwhelming urge to destroy. He drove a fist into Wes's stomach and had the satisfaction of seeing Wes crumble.

Todd, swearing, aimed a punch at Zach's face, but Zach blocked it and rammed both fists into the bigger man's chest even as he heaved upward.

The Lattigores sprawled to either side, enabling Zach to gain his hands and knees. But they were on him before he could rise any higher, Wes's spindly arms pinning his own to his side. Todd, the human wall, whipped a fist into Zach's ribs that spiked sheer agony. Gritting his teeth, Zach wrenched to one side in a gambit to throw Wes into Todd, but Wes clung to him like quicksand.

"Gonna pound you, boy," Todd reiterated.

Wes brayed like a mule.

Maybe it was the laugh. Maybe it was the feeling of helplessness. Maybe it was a reaction to years and years of bigotry. Whatever the cause, Zach's rage soared to new heights. In the grip of a seething reddish haze, he hurled himself at Todd, his head crashing into Todd's mouth and pulping Todd's lips like so much mush.

Swearing luridly, Todd backed off, shaking his head to clear it. Blood was spurting down over his chin.

No longer laughing, Wes tried to firm his hold. "I've got him, Todd! Don't worry! He won't get away!"

Zach had no intention of trying to. He butted Wes in the cheek, once, twice, three times, and finally Wes let go and fell, howling like a kicked dog. Zach was on him in a twinkling, hammering Wes hard, blow after blow, over and over. Wes feebly sought to defend himself, whimpering as his forearms were batted aside and his face and neck were mercilessly pummeled.

Todd leaped to his brother's aid. Gripping Zach's right wrist, he yanked, sending Zach stumbling. Zach recovered and pivoted as the barrel-chested Lattigore swept toward him. Sidestepping a left cross, Zach flicked a pair of swift jabs that barely fazed Todd but bought Zach the seconds needed to shift and stamp the heel of his foot onto Todd's shin. Bellowing, Todd delivered a backhand that narrowly missed.

So far no one had resorted to a weapon. Then, out of the corner of an eye, Zach glimpsed Wes clawing at a pistol. Bounding out of Todd's reach, Zach kicked at

Wes's hand, but Wes jerked back, fumbling with the flintlock. Zach sought to kick him again, but Todd sprang, tackling him and bearing him down.

Suddenly Zach found himself anchored at the ankles as the muzzle of a pistol was extended toward his face.

"Kill him!" one of the Lattigore women yipped in glee.

Minutes earlier, Louisa May Clark, little Susie Mills, and two other girls had reached the Platte. Lou, running her fingers through her hair, admired the brilliant sheen of the setting sun on a glistening pool. The breeze was picking up, as it usually did late in the day, rustling the nearby trees.

"Let's skip stones," one of the girls proposed.

Lou picked up a flat one the size of a walnut and hefted it several times before zinging it off across the river.

"Oh! It skipped five times! You're good!" Susie said, clapping her hands.

"See if any of you can beat me," Lou said.

They tried, but the best any of them could do was three skips. Still, they were having great fun.

Lou walked toward a rocky strip of shore where flat stones would be more plentiful. She was pleased things were going so well and had high hopes they could complete their journey without undue mishaps.

Being around the children was a special joy. Lou had often fantasized what it would be like to have sprouts of her own. Not the pregnancy part, because from what her mother and grandmother had said, morning sickness and being bloated like a pig's bladder weren't exactly pleasant experiences.

Lou liked to daydream about the kids she would have. About what they would be like, how they would look, how they'd behave. She flattered herself that her children would be perfect angels, that they wouldn't ever aggravate her, as she had seen other children do to their parents.

Now, as Lou gave Susie a stone suitable for skipping, she grinned at how much fun she would have with her own daughter one day. Doing things like this. Doing all the things her own mother had seldom had time to do with her. No matter what, Lou would always make time to play, to share, to be the best mother she could possibly be.

"Do you hear that, ma'am?" Susie unexpectedly asked, tugging at Lou's fingers.

Lou lifted her head and listened. A commotion had broken out. She heard the unmistakable sound of blows, of a scuffle, and Bertha Lattigore saying, "Get him! Show the lousy 'breed what's what!"

"Follow me!" Lou cried. She started to sprint to her beloved but drew up short. It wouldn't do to leave the young ones unattended. Not with cougars and grizzlies as common as fleas on a coon hound. Grating with frustration, she limited herself to moving as fast as they could, staying close to the water where the going was easiest.

"What is it?" Susie asked. "What's happening?"

"Is it more Indians?" another girl wondered in open terror. "Have they come to scalp us?"

"No," Lou said, wishing they had wings on their feet.

Hastening around the next bend, Lou saw Zach in the grasp of Todd Lattigore. Above them stood Wes, aiming a pistol. His intent was crystal clear. In reflex, Lou pointed her rifle, fixing a hasty bead on Wes Lattigore's arm, fixing to wound rather than slay, and fired. In her haste, she misjudged.

At the Hawken's crisp retort, Wes yelped and commenced swatting the air as if beset by bees. "My hand! My hand!"

The shot had struck his pistol, not him, jarring the flintlock loose but inflicting no serious harm.

Todd shoved upright, making a play for one of his

pistols, but Lou was quicker. Leveling her own, she stated flatly, "Try it and you die."

It was all Zach could do to keep from drawing his Bowie and ending it then and there. Slowly standing, boiling like an untended pot, he rubbed his sore jaw.

Once again the settlers converged from all points. Their penchant for having everyone talk at once resulted in rampant confusion until Orville Steinmuller arrived and hushed them. "Here, now!" he said when quiet reigned. "What's the meaning of this? What went on here, Mr. King?"

"Why don't you ask us?" Todd Lattigore snarled. "This damnable 'breed was trifling with our womenfolk!"

"Like hell," Zach said.

Wes couldn't stop flapping his hand. "He was! He was! We saw him with our own eyes!"

"All I did was ask if they had seen Lou," Zach told the growing group.

"Liar!" This from Verna Lattigore. "Red heathen liar! You waltzed up to us and insisted we go off in the bushes with you!"

Women gasped. Men grew somber. Frank Jensen, arriving on the scene, immediately seized the advantage. "See? I warned all of you, didn't I? I warned you what his kind is capable of!"

"Let's not rush to judgment," Orville said to calm them.

"Brother Steinmuller is eminently wise, as always," Jonathan Mathews interjected. "We should work this out in a civilized manner."

"Civilized?" Todd Lattigore practically snorted. "We're dealing with a half-breed! With an animal!"

Arguments were sparked, some siding with Zach, some siding with the affronted sisters and their husbands. It was then, at the height of the dispute, that Lou, unlimbering a pistol, marched over to her man and boldly hollered, "Quiet down, all of you!"

Silence, uneasy and strained, descended. Lightning bolts crackled in the eyes of the Lattigores as Lou confronted them. "The only liars here are you four. My fiancé would never be so crude."

"Be careful, girlie," Bertha said. "You shouldn't sass your elders. Riling us would be a mistake."

"Oh?" Lou pointed the flintlock at her. "And what, pray tell, will you do?"

Todd Lattigore stepped in front of Bertha. "I'm sick and tired of you waving firearms at people, wench. Keep it up and you'll pay, female or no female."

Zach was set to tear into the brothers again, but Orville Steinmuller interceded. Holding his arms aloft, Orville bawled, "Enough is enough! Frank, I want you to take your kin and go off by yourselves until they've cooled off."

Muttering, Jensen complied, but he was none too happy about it. Seizing his wife's arm, he hauled her off, the Lattigores trailing in their wake.

"I suggest doing the same," Orville told Zach and Lou. "There's been entirely too much bad blood between you and that clan. I'll grant it hasn't been your fault. But unless we can smooth things out, unless we can all get along, blood is liable to be spilled. And I don't want that."

"Amen, Brother," Jonathan Mathews said.

Zach retrieved his rifled and stalked westward, only vaguely aware of Louisa at his elbow. He was burning mad, madder than he had ever been, so mad he would gladly slit the throats of Jensen and the Lattigore brothers without a qualm. Twice now he had come to blows with them. Twice nothing had come of it other than a few scrapes and bruises. But the next time—and there *would* be one, as surely as night followed day—might be different. The third time they might do him grave harm, or worse.

Zach would rather have seen it settled, one way or

the other, than need to keep looking over his shoulder the rest of the journey. He would rather bring things to a head than have to tread on eggshells whenever Jensen and the Lattigores were around.

Louisa knew her betrothed's moods as well as she knew her own, and his posture told her he was in a funk. Anything she said or did would only serve to feed his anger. So she refrained from saying anything for the time being, content to dog his heels to a shadowed glade where he perched on a log and glumly rested his chin in his hands.

"I must have air between my ears."

"How do you figure?" Lou quizzed.

"To let you talk me into this harebrained notion. It's like sticking my head in a bear's mouth. I'm just asking for trouble."

"Think of the others, the ones who like us. Think of the children."

Zach preferred not to. He'd rather feed his rage, rather stay mad, so when he saw the Lattigores he'd make worm food of them on the spot.

"I recollect reading that Davy Crockett used to have a motto he lived by," Lou mentioned. "Always be sure you're right, then go ahead. Well, we're right in helping these people out. Now we have to go ahead. We have to do as we promised and get them to the mountains in one piece."

"You expect too much of me," Zach lamented.

"Do I? Maybe so. But only because I love you, and because I think you're the finest man I've ever met."

Zach's fury was fading despite his best effort. "I'm no better than anyone else," he protested.

"Oh? You're no better than Jensen or his cousins?" Lou challenged. "Do you hate white people just because they're white?"

"No," Zach begrudgingly admitted, although his opinion of his father's kind, by and large, wasn't flattering.

"Then you *are* better than vermin like them." Lou sat

and draped a slender arm across his wide shoulders. "Don't let them get your goat. We can see this through. Just as we'll see our marriage through. Have more faith in yourself."

Zach stared at her. Her knack for always looking at the bright side of things mystified him; hardship rolled off her like water off a duck's back. He chalked it up to the fact she hadn't had to deal with being looked down on simply because she was different, hadn't had to deal with the hatred he'd endured, month after month, year after year.

"What's that look for?" Lou asked.

"If you want me to see this through, I will."

"It's not what I want that counts. It's what *you* want." Lou had seen marriages where wives or husbands were forever bossing the other around, and marriages where one or the other connived to make their partner do as they wanted through clever manipulation, like a puppet-master working the strings of a puppet. She didn't care to have her union with Zach be anything like that. Theirs would be an honest, open marriage, where they could speak their piece and make their own decisions.

Zach had only one desire: to throw saddles on their mounts and head for the Rockies. But since Lou thought it right for them to stay, for her sake, he would. "All right. We'll see this through."

Smiling, Lou kissed his cheek. "I'm so proud of you right this moment. Your pa is always fond of saying Kings aren't quitters, and you're living proof."

Being compared to his father was the highest compliment Zach could think of. Embracing her, he molded his mouth to hers, the last of his anger evaporating like morning dew. When he straightened he was his old self, in complete control. "Sometimes you make me feel like I'm walking on clouds."

"Only sometimes?" Lou teased, and giggled.

They kissed again, Zach marveling that so lovely a creature had given her heart to him, that they would spend the rest of their lives together, always as blissful as they were then.

The twilight deepened. Neither was in any hurry to return. Zach stretched to relieve a kink in his spine, and as he arched his face into the breeze a faint scent registered, bringing him erect in a flash.

"What is it?" Lou inquired, surprised.

Zach turned his head to the right and the left, sniffing loudly, striving to pinpoint the odor's source. But it was present one second, gone the next, a phantom of the wind, defying detection. He moved to the Platte and scanned the other side, which was plunged in deep shadow.

Lou rose and joined him. She tested the air, too, but his senses were so much sharper than hers that whatever he smelled eluded her. "What is it?" she repeated.

The scent had vanished, leaving Zach to question whether it had really been there at all. Maybe it had been days-old urine, he persuaded himself. "That fracas with the Lattigores has me jumpy, I guess," he said, taking her hand. "Let's head back."

Lou spotted the first star of the evening and made a secret wish, a ritual of hers since she was knee-high to a lamb.

Zach continued to probe the opposite shoreline. High weeds and thick trees formed an inky wall impossible to penetrate. He titled his head, bothered by the conviction he shouldn't shrug it off, and inhaled deeply a few times.

"It can't be my perfume," Lou jested. "I haven't worn any since St. Louis."

There! Zach came to a halt. Across the river the vegetation was moving to the passage of a large form. Every nerve jangling, he waited for the cause to show itself.

The darkness deepened by the second. More stars sprouted as the firmament changed from sea blue to coal black. An eerie hush gripped the strip of woodland, and in that hush the the crunch of a dry twig was audible to both of them.

"Something is over there," Lou said.

"Come on." Zach pulled on her hand, breaking into a run. The thing on the other side was closer to their camp, closer to the settlers, closer to potential prey. They covered ten yards. Fifteen.

More crunching and rending of brush verified the beast was moving swiftly now, enticed by the noise the pilgrims were making. That, and the sweet aroma of sweaty horseflesh.

Lou succumbed to a chill that rippled down her spine. "Is that what I think it is?"

In response, Zach ran faster. He caught sight of a massive shape amid the rippling vegetation, barreling through it like a fur-clad battering ram. Ordinarily, the lords of the wilderness were much more stealthy, leading him to conclude this was a young one, one that had never had dealings with man. One that had no reason to fear guns or fire, rendering it doubly fearsome.

The pungent scent was stronger now, and Zach wasn't the only one who had caught wind of it. The strident nicker of a horse was the signal for others to whinny in rising alarm.

"Lord, no!" Lou exclaimed.

Ahead, a huge bristling monster burst from the tall weeds and into the river, sending up a spray that sparkled in the pale starlight. Without hesitation it cleaved toward the south bank, toward the ring of wagons.

Zach was flying like the wind, but it wasn't enough. The brute would reach their camp well before he could. Throwing back his head, he tried to warn the settlers by shouting at the top of his lungs. "Grizzly! Grizzly!"

As if on cue, the bear roared.

Chapter Five

Zach King and Louisa May Clark were still over fifty yards from camp when the first screams pierced the air. Strident yells and coarse bellows added to the confused din. A shot cracked, then others in a random volley. The bear roared a second time, only now the roar echoed pain and rising savagery. A high, hair-raising screech ended in a keening wail.

Zach ran for all he was worth, flying through the growth with no regard for his own safety. Ducking under a low limb, he reached the ring of wagons and sped between the foremost pair, then stopped short in consternation.

Lou caught up with him. She saw women and children running every which way, terrified mothers clutching distraught children, many screaming, some in tears. A man lay on his side in a crumpled heap. Tommy Baxter and others were hurriedly reloading rifles.

Zach didn't see the bear. For a second he thought maybe the shots had scared it off, but wavering whinnies from the horse string proved differently. He ran on out the far side of the circle, the Hawken tight against his shoulder.

The horses were in a worse panic than the settlers. They were neighing, rearing, kicking, and prancing. With ample cause. The young grizzly was in among them, its snarls part of the raucous racket. Suddenly the rope broke, or was severed, and horses began fleeing, running off into the night in blind confusion.

Zach tried to get a bead on the brute, but the milling animals hindered him. Attempting to move closer, he was nearly bowled over by a fleeing stallion.

Lou, worried he would be trampled, grabbed his arm and yanked him back. "Wait until they stop stampeding!"

The bear's immense bulk was at the center of the whirlwind of movement. A front paw rose and fell; a horse uttered a humanlike shriek. The bear lunged, and bone crunched with a rending snap.

Zach angled to the left, desperate for a clear shot, the frenzied horses again thwarting him. He lost sight of the grizzly. "Stay put," he hollered at Lou, and did the exact opposite, throwing himself into the melee. Frightened horses bore down on him. He dodged one way, then another. He couldn't avoid them all, though, and the shoulder of a sorrel clipped him. Tottering, he didn't go down.

"Zach, don't!" Lou attempted to go after him and pull him to safety, but a couple of stallions flew between them, forcing her back.

Some of the horses were still tied together, quaking in their tracks. Others snorted and plunged in an effort to join their brethren in flight.

Zach came to where he had last seen the bear, only it wasn't there. An object in the grass drew his attention, and he bent over it. The foreleg of a horse had been ripped from the animal's body. The horse it had been attached to, however, was gone. Crushed grass smeared by dark stains explained its absence. The grizzly had dragged it off into the bushes.

Impulsively, Zach took a few steps in pursuit, then came to his senses. The horse was beyond saving, and grizzlies were notoriously testy about having their meals interrupted. Were he to blunder into the brush, he was bound to be attacked. Resigned to the loss, he surveyed the string.

Fully half the animals had fled. Eight or nine of the loose ones had stayed nearby and were moving back and forth in confusion, their nostrils flared, their ears pricked. The darkness made it hard to determine if any had been hurt, but one was limping and another, still tethered, was on the ground, froth rimming its mouth.

Some of the farmers rushed up, their rifles at the ready. "Where the devil is the fiend?" Silas Kern excitedly asked. "Where did it go?"

"Off to eat its supper," Zach said.

Tommy Baxter gestured. "Shouldn't we go after it? What if it comes back in the middle of the night?"

"It won't," Zach answered. He had more than a passing familiarity with the habits of silvertips. The griz would gorge itself, feasting until it couldn't take another bite, then find a spot to sleep off the stupor.

Todd Lattigore angrily swore. "You don't know that for sure! I say we hunt the thing down now, before it gets too far!"

Zach nodded at the murky undergrowth. "Go ahead. Charge on in there. And after the grizzly comes out of nowhere and tears you limb from limb, we'll bury the bits and pieces that are left."

"What would you have us do?" Tommy Baxter inquired. "Nothing?"

"Round up as many of the horses as you can," Zach directed. "We'll go after the rest at dawn."

"What about Orville?" Silas Kern remarked.

"What about him?"

"Didn't you see him on the ground back there?"

Zach remembered the man lying in the circle. Without another word, he raced back into the ring of firelight. A dozen others had beaten him there, and he had to shoulder through them to reach Steinmuller.

The oldster was on his back, his hands at his sides. Deathly white, he was conscious but weak. His homespun shirt had been slashed by oversized claws and blood was dampening the wool. "I'm fine," he was softly protesting. "Give me a bit to catch my breath and I'll be able to stand."

Agatha was there, clasping his hand. "You'll do no such thing, husband. Lie still while we carry you into our wagon."

"Really, all this fuss is unnecessary," Orville said.

Kneeling, Zach leaned forward. "Let us be the judge of that. He gingerly parted the shorn fabric to examine the wounds. Four long gashes were mute testimony to the grizzly's ferocity. Fortunately, its oversized claws had only scraped Steinmuller's ribs, not penetrating into his vital organs.

"It was my own fault," Orville commented. "I heard someone call out and turned." He winced, then groaned. "The bear was almost on top of me. I couldn't get out of its way fast enough."

"You can't blame yourself," Zach said. If anyone was at fault, he mused, it was him, for not being there. Of all of them, he would have had the best chance of stopping the griz before it reached the string.

Someone else thought so, too. "Where in hell were you?" Frank Jensen demanded. "We're paying good money to have you guide and protect us, yet when we really need you, you're nowhere around."

"Let him alone," Agatha Steinmuller said. "He can't be everywhere at once. And the way that bear came at us, there's nothing anyone could have done." Placing her hands flat, she rose. "Now, who's going to help carry my husband?"

Working in concert, exercising the utmost care, five

men bore Orville to the Steinmullers' wagon and placed him on a special bed of blankets Agatha had arranged. She promptly shooed them out, allowing only Tamar Mathews to remain to help her clean and bandage the gashes.

No one else had been harmed, a small miracle in itself. Once, years ago, Zach had visited a Crow village shortly after a grizzly had gone amok. The bear had been shot with an arrow by a warrior who spied it a stone's throw from the lodges. Four Crows were slain, twice as many wounded, before the beast was driven off.

The settlers were too excited to sleep. Zach instructed them to pile logs on the fires until the circle was lit as if it were broad daylight. All the horses were brought into the ring and a tally made of those that were missing.

Toward midnight the camp quieted. The children were ushered to bed, the fires allowed to burn lower. Guards were posted, shifts set up so that every man would take a turn before morning.

Having done all he could, Zach wearily returned to the Steinmullers' wagon. Lou and he always spread out their blankets next to it at night, and she was there, waiting.

"About time."

"Baxter is supposed to wake me in a couple of hours, so I'd better get right to sleep," Zach mentioned, sinking down with a sigh. Reclining on his back, he laced his fingers under his head and idly gazed at the myriad of stars sparkling in the firmament.

"You don't want to talk?"

"About what?"

Louisa slid nearer and lowered her voice so neither of the Steinmullers would overhear. "About the difference between butterflies and moths," she said sarcastically. "Don't try to brush me off. I know you. I know you'll hold yourself to account over Orville."

"I shouldn't have strayed off like I did," Zach allowed.

"You were walking off steam," Lou reminded him. "Anyone would have done the same after how the Lattigores treated you."

Zach placed his left forearm across his eyes. "Can't we talk about this tomorrow? It's been a long day."

"Avoid the issue if you want. But remember. You can no more control events that you can the weather."

"I'll keep that in mind," Zach said, rolling over so his back was to her. But she wouldn't take the hint.

"I went through the same thing, you know. When my pa was killed, I blamed myself. I tormented myself day in and day out for not doing something to save him. Yet the truth is, there's nothing I could have done. Those hostiles had us dead to rights. They'd have rubbed me out, too, if they hadn't discovered I was a female."

"This was different."

"How, exactly?"

"The hostiles had you and your pa surrounded. You had nowhere to run, nowhere to hide. If you'd lifted a finger against them, they'd have turned you into a pincushion." Zach lowered his arm to look at her. "If I'd been here, I could have stopped the bear. I've killed grizzlies before, remember?"

Lou would never forget. It had been the day they met. Like father, like son, apparently, since Nate King's Indian name, bestowed on him by a Cheyenne chief, was Grizzly Killer. Nate liked to say that the only reason he'd earned his reputation was that he was one of the first whites to call the mountains home, and back then the mighty bears were much more plentiful.

Shifting, Lou rested her cheek on Zach's chest. "Just don't try to be like Atlas. Don't bear the weight of the world on your shoulders."

"Like who?"

Lou's mother had been fond of reading to her each night before she went to bed, the ancient Greek myths being her mother's favorites. "I'll rustle up a book about him the next time we visit civilization."

Which would be never, if Zach had any say. He'd experienced enough of big cities and towns to last him a decade. The hectic pace of life, the rude people, the carriage traffic, the utter bedlam were more than he was willing to bear. Give him an orderly, tranquil Shoshone village any day.

Lou wasn't upset when he didn't reply. He got that way now and then. "Remember, too, I talked you into this. The responsibility is as much mine as it is yours." When he still wouldn't respond, she shut her eyes and let herself drift off.

Zach wanted to do the same. He was tired enough to sleep a good twelve hours, but his mind was racing like an antelope. He thought of his folks, and how much he missed them, and of his pain-in-the-tush sister, Evelyn, and how he sort of missed her. He dwelled on the Shoshones and how he would like to visit them next summer, how great it would be to see old friends and go on raids and buffalo hunts.

Adrift in himself, Zach lost track of time, so much so that when a hand fell on his shoulder and Tommy Baxter whispered his name, he said, "What's wrong?"

"It's your turn to stand watch."

The hours had whisked by. Zach slowly slid out from under Lou, who was sound asleep, and gently lowered her onto the blanket, covering her with another.

"It's been pretty quiet," Baxter whispered. "Jacob Marsh claimed he heard something growl earlier, but Mathews and I didn't. And nothing ever showed. The horses are bedded down and most everyone else is in dreamland."

Zach scooped up his Hawken. "Go turn in." Yawning, he took a circuit of the Conestogas. On the south side, Kern was on guard. To the east a fellow known as Wilson was leaning against a wagon, struggling to stay alert. Both had just come on and were not very enthusiastic about it.

"That critter is long gone," Wilson complained. "Having three of us stay up is a waste when only one man need do the job."

"We can't afford to lose anymore horses," Zach said. Actually, they could, since the Ohioans had been smart enough to bring few extra animals along, but it was better than telling Wilson he was a lazy so-and-so.

Zach's post was along the northern edge of the encampment, closest to the Platte and to the vegetation. In the adjacent trees an owl voiced the eternal query of its kind, while off on the prairie coyotes yipped in canine chorus. Otherwise, the night was undisturbed.

To ward off lingering tendrils of drowsiness, Zach paced awhile. The air was crisp, invigorating, a stiff breeze swaying the grass and leaves. As he stood there in the shadow of a wagon and gazed around the camp, the enormity of the task he had taken on hit with the force of a physical blow. He imagined all the sleeping settlers, all the women and all those innocent little children, whose lives were, in effect, in his hands.

As the incident with the grizzly had demonstrated, protecting them every minute of every day wasn't humanly possible. Had he bitten off more than he could chew? Zach asked himself. What made him think he was man enough to follow in his father's footsteps? Orville being hurt was bad enough. What if it had been one of the women or children? He'd never forgive himself. It would be the same as if it happened to his own ma or sister.

Zach glanced toward the horses just as his bay raised its head and peered past him, its ears rising. Swiveling, he scanned the bordering foliage and the murky ribbon of water beyond. If something was out there, it wasn't showing itself.

Another horse stirred.

Zach sidled up against the wagon so he would be harder to spot. He'd been confident the grizzly wouldn't return, but bears could be as contrary as females. He could well be wrong.

A thump off to the right brought Zach around in a crouch, his thumb curling back the rifle's hammer. Deep in the gloom something moved, something big, coming directly toward the circle. He pressed his check to the stock, eager for a clear shot, for a chance to bring the bruin down. Then he saw another large silhouette, and a third.

It was extremely rare for grizzlies to travel in groups, unless it was a female with cubs, and the creatures Zach saw were much too large to be the latter. Puzzled, he waited expectantly for whatever they were to show themselves.

A soft nicker caused Zach to let out the breath he hadn't realized he was holding. The trio emerged from the woods, their tails swishing lazily. Halting, the leader stomped a hoof.

"Good boy, good boy," Zach said softly, leaning the rifle against the Conestoga. Having several horses return on their own was encouraging. Maybe others would, too, saving the men a lot of work on the morrow.

The animals were exhausted and offered no resistance. Zach led them to the string and added them, then checked on the other two sentries. Kern was awake, but Wilson was perched on a wagon tongue, his chin on his chest, dozing. When Zach prodded him, the settler leaped up as if his clothes were ablaze and wildly swung his rifle from side to side.

"What? What is it? What's going on?"

"You were asleep," Zach said.

Wilson wasn't the sort to apologize. "Can you blame me? I was up since first light, not a wink of rest all day, and you have the gall to expect me to get by with two measly hours?"

"You'll get two more after we're relieved."

"Which won't be near enough," Wilson griped.

"We're each taking turns," Zach said. "I can't be anymore fair than that." He walked off before the man provoked him into saying something rash. The prairie was uncommonly still, the coyotes and the owl long since silent. Even the breeze had died, leaving the trees as motionless as statues. A shooting star streaked a fiery path across the heavens, a rare sight that never failed to fascinate him.

The fires were so low, they were almost out. Zach decided to replenish the one at his end of camp, but the wood collected earlier had been used up. Venturing into the vegetation, he searched for downed limbs. They were difficult to find, but he came across a couple that were suitable. As he moved toward a knot of cottonwoods, a strong feeling came over him, a troubling sensation that he was being watched. Halting, he studied the growth.

Zach didn't discount his feeling. Not when similar sensations had saved his hide before. "Always trust your instincts," his pa had taught him when he was a boy, and his pa had, as always, been right.

It had been a mistake to look for wood without informing someone. Zach should have told one of the farmers what he was about. Now he was on his own, twenty yards from the circle and safety, with who-knew-what lurking in the dimness.

It must be the bear, Zach figured. The grizzly had eaten its fill of the mare, but instead of going off to sleep had come back to wreak more havoc. Or maybe it was merely curious about the whites and their wagons. Whichever, the big question was whether it would permit Zach to retreat unmolested.

Zach held onto the firewood. To drop it might provoke the bear, might make it think he was up to something and cause it to hurtle from ambush. Slowly backpedaling, Zach examined every shadow, every nook. He almost missed the telltale hint of motion adjacent to a briar patch.

That was when Zach spied the eyes. A pair of slanted greenish orbs down low to the ground, dimly mirroring the feeble glow from the fading campfire. They were fixed on him in total concentration, unblinking, as if carved from stone.

A painter, Zach guessed. It had to be. The eyes were the wrong shape and size to be those of the grizzly. They belonged to a big cat, to the biggest there was, a roving cougar lured by the tantalizing scent of the doomed mare's blood.

Ordinarily, the reclusive cats avoided contact with humans. Nine times out of ten, they would run the other way. It was the tenth time a person had to worry about. Some cougars, like people, were born vicious, and would as soon dine on human flesh as on venison.

Zach hoped this one wasn't one of them. He had the fallen limbs under his left arm, the Hawken in his right hand. If the cougar sprang, he'd be hard-pressed to level a gun quickly enough to stop it.

"What are you doing, Mr. King?"

Stupefied, Zach turned partway around—just enough to see the sprite who had come up unnoticed and still keep an eye on the predator. "What on earth are you doing here, girl?" he demanded.

Little Susie Mills had on a nightshirt that fell to her ankles. Her feet were bare, her hair disheveled. "I was thirsty, so I got up for some water and saw you walk off."

"You shouldn't have followed me," Zach said, tensing as the pair of eyes in the brush began to rise.

"What are you doing out here by yourself?"

"Fetching firewood," Zach explained. The eyes had vanished, blinking out as if they never existed, which meant the cat was on the move.

"Can I help?" the girl offered.

"No." Zach stepped in front of her to put himself between her and the cougar. "I want you to head back. Look straight ahead and don't stop no matter what."

"What's wrong? You sound upset."

Out of the mouths of babes, Zach reflected. "Nothing is wrong. It's not safe to roam about at night, is all."

"But you're here," Susie said. "I'm safe as can be."

Zach knew she believed that because he had saved her when she strayed off. In her childish view, that made him special. Nudging her with an elbow to hasten her along, he coaxed, "Don't dawdle."

"What's your hurry?" Susie balked. "I like it at night."

"So do I," Zach said. "But I have to keep the fire going, and it's almost out. We need to add this wood."

"Why didn't you say so?" Susie tugged on his buckskin shirt. "Let me help. My ma has me tote wood all the time."

Zach's skin prickled. He glanced up, afraid he had let down his guard and the cat would be on them in another heartbeat, but the only motion now was the stirring of leaves as the breeze waxed stronger.

"Ma says I'm getting to be a big girl," Susie prattled on. "I know how to cook, how to sew."

"I bet your mother is very proud of you," Zach said. He couldn't spy the cougar anywhere and chided himself for being so nervous. Plainly, it had traipsed off to parts unknown. Good riddance, he thought, and grinned.

"What's that, Mr. King?" Susie asked, pointing.

The painter was on a low, thick limb not ten feet to the north, its legs curled as if about to leap.

Every muscle and sinew in Zach's body tensed. "When I tell you, I want you to run as fast as you can to your wagon. Don't stop. Don't look back."

"Is this a game? I like games."

"If you want. I'll race you to see who gets there first," Zach said. "On the count of three." He paused and faced the cougar. "One."

Susie tittered and hopped up and down. "This will be fun!"

"Two," Zach said. The cougar would probably leap the moment the girl bolted, and he'd do all he could to keep it at bay until she was out of harm's way. The flintlocks were his best bet. At close range, the pistols were as effective as the long gun.

"I'm ready," Susie declared.

Zach didn't take his gaze off the lion. It hadn't moved, but its long tail was flicking like a bullwhip. "Remember, don't stop for anything," he said, then barked out, "Three! Go, Susie! Go!"

The child did as she was bid, running with all the speed her stubby legs could muster. Instantly, Zach dropped the branches and the Hawken and stabbed both hands at his pistols. Sweeping them from under his wide brown leather belt, he brought both to bear on the cougar—only it wasn't there. It had risen and leaped, but not toward him, *away* from him, and away from Susie Mills. In a lithe arc it cleared the tree, alighted on all fours, and with incredible swiftness melted into the dark.

Zach trained the flintlocks on where the painter vanished, unwilling to credit his good fortune. He half dreaded the cat would loop around to reach Susie or to come at him from another angle. But as the seconds passed and it didn't reappear, he allowed himself the luxury of a smile.

The painter was gone! Zach placed the flintlocks back under his belt and snatched up the Hawken. He had been lucky, luckier than anyone had a right to be. His blunder in entering the woods might well have cost a child her life. Pivoting, he took a stride, then stopped cold.

Susie was four feet off, her hands on her hips.

"What's the matter?" Zach inquired.

"You didn't run. You tricked me." She wagged a finger. "You're mean, Mr. King. Mean, mean, mean."

Zach couldn't help himself. He laughed out loud.

Chapter Six

Collecting the horses wasn't quite the chore Zach envisioned. Most hadn't strayed very far, no more than a mile or so, and were rounded up before midmorning. By noon all but three were accounted for, and Zach announced that their westward journey could resume.

"Hold on, there," Frank Jensen said.

Jensen had been among the six members of Zach's search party, but much to Zach's surprise hadn't given him a lick of grief until now.

"One of those animals is mine, a sorrel I'm right fond of. I say we keep hunting for another hour, at least."

Everyone within earshot glanced at Zach. To refuse might give them the idea he was doing it to spite the man, so, against his better judgment, Zach responded, "Another hour. But no more. If we haven't found your sorrel by then, we never will."

Jensen touched the brim of his hat. "I'm obliged, King," he said, calling Zach by his name for the first time since they met.

Twenty minutes later, they topped a knoll to find not

only the sorrel grazing below, but the other missing horses, as well.

Still, it was early afternoon before the wagons rolled westward again. To make up for some of the lost time, Zach didn't call a halt until the sun dipped to the horizon. Learning from his previous mistake, he instructed the settlers to tether their stock *inside* the circle from then on out. The horses were divided in half and tied close to the wagons, leaving an open space in the middle.

The pilgrims were in good spirits, relieved the grizzly's attack had cost them only a marc. Orville Steinmuller would be bedridden for a week to ten days, but he would fully recover. That night they sat around the fires, laughing and joking. Even the Lattigores and Jensen were in fine fettle.

Zach didn't join in. He was off by himself on the north side of the camp, cleaning his rifle, when Lou detached herself from a group of women and traipsed over

"It wouldn't kill you to mingle."

Shrugging, Zach replied, "In case you haven't noticed, a few of the men aren't as fond of me as the ladies are of you."

"You're forgetting Bertha and Verna," Lou said. "They'd as soon toss me off a cliff as look at me." She sat down and watched him wrap a small piece of cloth around the end of his ramrod and shove it down the Hawken's barrel. "Want to do mine when you're done? It's been a month of Sundays since I bothered."

Most mountaineers were rather lax in keeping their guns clean. Zach was more meticulous, in part thanks to his father, who had impressed on him at an early age that a filthy rifle or a dull knife could prove costly. "Only if you'll give me a back rub afterward."

Lou grinned. "What is it about back rubs you love so much? I swear, you'll wear my fingers down to stubs if I keep giving you one every time I turn around."

"They relax me," Zach said. They melted his tension away like butter under a hot sun. For a short while he forgot his cares and woes and simply enjoyed being alive.

"But one a day?" Lou teased.

"Ten would be better, but I'll take what I can get."

Chuckling, Lou placed a hand on his head and ruffled his raven hair. She sorely desired to go off alone with him for a spell, to have a day all to themselves, but until the wagon train reached the Rockies that was out of the question, barring a miracle.

"Mind if we join you folks?"

Lou hadn't noticed Tommy Baxter and his lovely wife, Elizabeth. They were hand in hand, both exhibiting signs of being slightly nervous.

"We'd like to talk to you," Tommy said, "about life in the mountains."

"If it's all right," Elizabeth said quickly, looking at Zach.

Lou gestured. "Plant yourselves and ask away." She bubbled with glee that they were being so friendly. Normally, even the outgoing Tamar Mathews and Agatha Steinmuller were hesitant about chatting with her when Zach was around. "What would you like to know?"

Elizabeth primly sank down, folding her hands in her lap. "Everything. All we have to go by is hearsay. But you two have lived up there. You know what it's like for real."

Tommy sat cross-legged and rested his elbows on his knees. "The thing that has me most concerned is how dangerous it is."

Zach extracted the ramrod. "The wilderness is always dangerous. Never take it for granted or it will take your life."

"What's the worst danger of all?" Tommy wanted to know.

"Stupidity."

"I'm serious."

"So am I," Zach said. "Stupidity has killed more people than all the hostile Indians and grizzlies combined." He could cite scores of examples. Such as the mountaineer who had gone out on the bitterly cold winter's day to gather firewood, dressed only in a buckskin shirt and leggings, and froze to death when he slipped on ice and broke his leg and couldn't make it back to his cabin. Or the trapper who caught his own hand in a bear trap and had to hack it off with an ax to free himself, only to bleed dry and die. Then there was the greenhorn who had entered a Blackfoot village mistaking them for harmless Flatheads. And on and on he could go.

"We all do dumb things from time to time," Tommy Baxter said. "It can't be helped."

"It can if you think about what you're doing before you do it," Zach said.

Lou cleared her throat. "One of the most important lessons to learn is to always be on the lookout. Never leave your cabin without a weapon. Never stray far unless you tell each other where you're going. Little things like that can make all the difference in the world."

Elizabeth faced her. "Doesn't it get to you? Always being on edge, I mean? I'll be a nervous wreck after only a month."

"No, you won't," Lou assured her, "because you'll grow used to doing things a certain way. To always strapping on a gun or knife first thing in the morning. To always looking out the window before you open the door. To always looking and listening before you go into the forest. Things like that."

"I should think it would make me old before my time," Elizabeth said.

Tommy reached for her hand. "We can still turn around and go back to St. Louis, my love. If you're having second thoughts, now is the time to tell me."

"No. We've come this far, we'll go the rest of the way," Elizabeth stated. "Besides, this is your dream come true. I don't want to spoil it."

Zach had to ask a question that had pricked at him like a thorn since the day he met them. "Why the Rockies?" he inquired. "Why did you pick there to live, of all places?" Whatever motivated them might motivate others, bringing swarms of whites to the high country.

Tommy leaned back. "A lot of factors, actually. The land is there for the taking, so it won't cost us a cent. And we'll be free to live as we please. No one will be looking over our shoulders, telling us what we can and can't do."

"But acreage is cheap all along the frontier," Zach noted, as he'd seen for himself on his recent visit to St. Louis. "And living there is a lot safer."

"Cheap, yes, but not free," Tommy reiterated. "In the mountains I can claim all the land I want and no one can object."

"Except the tribe whose territory you're in," Zach remarked.

"We'll make peace with them," Tommy said. "We'll trade with them for the right to till the soil. Surely they won't mind?"

"It depends on the tribe. The Utes tried to drive my pa out for years and only stopped after he befriended one of their chiefs."

"What about the Shoshones?" Elizabeth asked. "Didn't Louisa say they're the nicest tribe anywhere? What's to stop us from living near them?"

"Nothing," Zach conceded, "except that they live close to Blackfoot territory, so you're more likely to be raided."

Elizabeth's features clouded. "Are the Blackfeet really as awful as everyone claims? Do they honestly hate whites with a passion?"

"They kill whites on sight," Zach declared.

"But why? What did we ever do to them?"

Zach replaced the ramrod in its housing under the Hawken's barrel. "The whole thing started with the Louis and Clark expedition. Meriwether Louis and some of his men killed a Blackfoot who was trying to steal from them, and the tribe has held it against whites ever since."

"How unfair."

Zach uncapped his powder horn. "There's more to it than that. The Blackfeet are a powerful tribe, and they don't like anyone to intrude on their territory. That includes the Shoshones, the Flatheads, the Crows, you name it. To a Blackfoot, everyone is their enemy."

"Except the Bloods and the Piegans," Lou said.

"Who?" Tommy asked.

"Allies of the Blackfeet, part of the Blackfoot Confederacy, as the whites call it," Zach answered. "They control the northern plains from the Missouri into Canada. But don't worry. We'll stay well shy of them."

Tommy gnawed on his lower lip. "We've heard tales of Indian atrocities. Tell me true. What would the Blackfeet really do if they caught my wife and me?"

"Her they might keep, if a warrior were to take a fancy to her," Zach said. "As for you, they'd start by tying you to a stake. Maybe gouge out your eyes and remove your tongue, chop off your fingers and toes. Then they'd gut you and pull out your intestines for the scavengers to eat. Before they were done, the suffering would drive you mad."

Tommy Baxter's throat bobbed. "They'd do all that?"

"Or worse."

"What could possibly be worse?"

Elizabeth held up a hand. "I don't want to know! Please! I've heard more than enough. It'll give me nightmares."

Two figures came toward them, Jonathan Mathews and his wife. "Don't let it trouble you, Sister," the Quaker said. "Have faith in our Maker and He will preserve you."

"Faith won't ward off arrows and lances," Zach commented.

"On the contrary," Mathews said. "Our faith is our

buckler, our shield. When hostiles assault us, we're to turn the other cheek. So long as I live, I refuse to lift a finger against my fellow man."

Zach didn't mince words. "Then you won't live long." He was perplexed when Lou slapped his arm.

"Whether I do or not is irrelevant," Mathews said. "It's not how long we live but *how* we live that counts. In total obedience to God. Treating all men as our brothers, all women as our sisters."

Tamar Mathews beamed. "My husband and I aren't afraid to die, Brother King. We know that we'll go onto our just reward."

The astonishing thing to Zach was that they were completely sincere. He'd met people like them before, whites who put their religion above all else, and frankly, he didn't quite know what to make of them. What good was their faith if it earned them an early grave? His father's outlook made more sense: be neighborly, but always keep a loaded gun handy.

"Don't let his stories scare either of you," the Quaker told the Baxters. "Brother Steinmuller has it all planned out. We'll invite the Indians to visit our valley and offer them a share in our bounty if they'll give us their word that they'll let us live in peace."

"That won't work with the Blackfeet or their allies," Zach said. He also doubted it would appease the Utes, who controlled a sizable chunk of the southern Rockies.

"I can't say as I can commend your attitude, Brother King," Jonathan Mathews said. "We won't know until we try."

"And by then you could be lying in the dirt with a lance through your chest."

Tamar came to her husband's defense. "Why must you be so negative?"

"I'm not. I'm being realistic."

"But if everyone thought like you do, the human race would never get along," Tamar rebutted. "It's been my experience that when people make a special effort to be kind, others respond *in* kind. Spiritually, we're all brothers and sisters, remember."

Zach refrained from laughing in her face. He didn't deny that the pair were as kind as could be. But if they walked up to, say, an Apache or a Comanche, and smiled, and called the warrior their brother, they'd be in for the shock of their lives. Jonathan would be dead before he knew what hit him. Then the warrior would drag Tamar back to his lodge and do things to her that would outrage her spiritual sensibilities. "With all respect, Mrs. Mathews, you and your husband have a lot to learn."

Jonathan chuckled. "This from someone half our age? Trust me, son. Brother Steinmuller's plan will deliver us from evil. The Lord, after all, works in mysterious ways."

"Mighty mysterious," Zach admitted, because for the life of him he couldn't comprehend how the God of the whites could be so filled with love and compassion, as all the Bible-thumpers claimed, when He allowed people to go around butchering and slaughtering one another.

Mathews's brow puckered. "Tell me, Brother King. You're not, by any chance, a heathen at heart, are you?"

"If you're asking me if I've fully accepted the white man's religion," Zach said, "the answer is no, I haven't. Oh, my pa tried his best. He used to read from the Good Book to my sister and me each and every day. He wanted us to believe as he does. But I can't honestly say I do."

"Oh, my," Tamar said, stunned.

"It saddens me, Brother King," Jonathan said, "to learn you have deprived yourself of the greatest joy mortal man can know."

Zach's idea of joy was spending an hour cuddling with Lou, but he didn't deem it appropriate to mention as much. "Maybe one day I'll get it all worked out in my head. Until then, if God is as understanding as everyone says, he can hardly blame me for being a mite confused."

Tamar patted his arm. "Rest easy. By the time we reach the mountains, my husband and I will have you on the straight and narrow."

"That reminds me," Elizabeth Baxter said. "How soon after we arrive can we send for a minister? Orville gave me the impression it would be next spring."

"Possibly," Jonathan said. "Although with all we have to do, building a church by then might not be feasible. But by next fall at the very latest."

Zach stifled more amusement. The settlers weren't even to the Rockies yet and already they had big plans to bring in a man of the cloth. Talk about putting the cart before the horse! By next fall most or all of them could well be dead. "I need to stretch my legs," he said, rising, and moved toward the horses.

"I'll join you," Lou offered. When they had gone halfway, she whispered. "What's wrong? I could tell something was bothering you."

"They're fools."

"Hush. What if they hear? You'll hurt their feelings."

"Why is it white people always think others should see the world as they do?"

"They didn't say that."

Zach halted at the string and patted a sorrel. "Weren't you listening? They think all they have to do is welcome every Indian that comes along with open arms and the Indians will spare them from harm. But we both know better, don't we?"

Louisa couldn't argue, not when her own father had fallen victim to a war party.

"And such big plans they have!" Zach said irritably. "A church! Their next step, likely as not, will be to build a school. Before long, a town will sprout. More and more people will come and the town will grow into a city. Give them ten years and whites will overrun the mountains just as they've overrun all the land between the Atlantic Ocean and the Mississippi River."

"You're making a mountain out of a molehill."

"Am I? Whites are like locusts. They devour everything in their path."

It bothered Louisa when he talked about her kind that way. "Yet you're marrying one of those locusts," she reminded him, playfully jabbing his ribs with her elbow. "So you must like bugs more than you're letting on."

Zach fell silent. He'd witnessed so many changes because of the whites, and few for the better. Thanks to them the beaver were nearly extinct, the mountain buffalo had dwindled to near nothing, and entire villages had been decimated by white disease. Small wonder talking about it raised his hackles.

Zach had to bear in mind that just as there were good and bad Indians, so were there good whites and ones who were not so good. And Louisa fell firmly into the former category. "I always liked to study insects when I was little," he said. "You remind me of a praying mantis I kept for a while."

"I do, huh?"

"Yep. Those long legs. Those big eyes. And your pincers—"

"I'll pinch you," Lou said, and did so, squeezing his upper arm as hard as she could. "Some fiancé you are! Comparing the woman you're marrying to a mantis."

"Would you rather I compared you to a dung beetle?" Zach quipped, and received another pinch.

Laughing, they hugged, and as they separated, Zach glimpsed Frank Jensen and Jensen's cousins glaring at them from over by a fire. His good mood was ruined. Glaring back, he grasped Lou's hand and walked around the string, putting the horses between them and the bigots.

Lou couldn't help but notice the change that came over him. Scanning the encampment, she spied the reason. "Don't let them get to you, handsome."

"I can't help it," Zach said. It had always been thus,

since he was a boy and a trader at a rendezvous had referred to him as a "bratty 'breed."

"So what if they give us dirty looks? They haven't bothered us since your fight with the Lattigores. I think they've learned their lesson."

Zach didn't share her confidence. The only thing the Lattigores had learned was that he was tougher than they had reckoned. They'd jump him again eventually.

As if that wasn't enough to keep Zach on edge, soon they would be at the southern fringe of territory claimed by the most fierce warriors on the plains. With a little luck they might make it through. But he had to be extra vigilant from then on out or all their lives were forfeit.

Another week went by. A week of plodding progress, with Zach casting repeated longing looks westward. He regretted ever agreeing to act as scout, but shielded his regret from Lou for fear she would think poorly of him.

For Lou's part, it was a week of fun and pleasantries. The children had taken a special shine to her, and on their noon breaks and in the evening the girls invited her to play games like tag and hide-and-seek.

It made Lou think of her own childhood, which hadn't been all that long ago. Of the cousins and friends she had been close to, some of whom later betrayed her trust in St. Louis when they tried to keep her from "throwing her life away," as her aunt put it, by wedding Zach. To stop her, they'd even gone so far as to try and have him killed.

Yet although she had suffered the soul-searing barbs of bald treachery and rank deceit, Lou refused to view the world as Zach did. She positively refused to believe that most people were prejudiced. Nor would she mistrust everyone she met until they had proven worthy of her trust. Her philosophy was to extend the hand of friendship to one and all, and if it was slapped away, then act accordingly.

Consequently, Lou became good friends with many

of the women, particularly Agatha and Molly. Tamar, of course, was always as sweet as fresh-baked apple pie, a result, Lou figured, of Tamar's Quaker upbringing. Elizabeth Baxter, Helen Marsh, Martha Kern, they were likewise as open and nice as could be.

So it wasn't uncommon for Lou to sit and talk with them until late at night, until their husbands were nagging them to turn in and the women were so tired they could hardly keep their eyes open.

Lou came to realize that, unlike her betrothed, she was sincerely glad the settlers were going to the Rockies. It would give her someone to visit whenever she felt the need to mingle with her own kind. But she didn't mention her feelings to Zach, given how touchy he was on the subject.

There were moments—fleeting moments, to be sure, and few and far between—when Lou questioned whether she was doing the right thing by marrying him. They were so different, both in backgrounds and temperament. She fretted she would make him miserable, that years down the road their special bond might fade.

Then, one afternoon, as she was riding beside the Mathewses' wagon chatting with Tamar, Zach came riding back to inform her he was going on ahead to scout.

"Again?" Lou said. "You've gone off four times today. Why so often?"

"I take my job seriously," Zach said a trifle testily. Reining his bay around, he galloped to the northwest without once glancing back and waving as he routinely did.

"Men!" Lou said.

Tamar chortled. "They can be a trial, can't they? Makes you wonder why the Good Lord saw fit to shackle us with them." Her husband, seated beside her, ignored the barb.

Lou looked at the older woman. "Did you ever have doubts? About marrying, I mean?"

"Sister, every woman has doubts. It's only normal.

Any of them who claim otherwise are liars."

"Did you have doubts about Jonathan?"

Tamar looked at him affectionately. "Enough to fill a silo. He wasn't the handsomest man I'd ever seen, and his table manners were atrocious."

Lou laughed.

"I spent hours worrying, day in and day out. It got so bad, I gave myself headaches. Was he the right one? Could I stay with him my whole life long? Would we be happy? Or would we constantly bicker and fight like some couples do? Oh, I went around and around with myself. All because I was too young to have learned the great truth."

"What great truth?" Lou said, all interest.

"That the parts go to make up the whole. And when the parts can't agree, we have to go with the part that matters most."

"I don't follow you."

"Ever taken a good look at yourself in a mirror? What did you see? A woman. A whole woman. But you have parts that go to make up that whole. Your mind, your soul, your heart, your body." Tamar fiddled with her bonnet. "Sometimes those parts don't agree on things. That's when we give ourselves a lot of needless grief."

Lou waited for her to go on.

"Take Jonathan as an example. In my mind I had all sorts of doubts. I ran myself in circles fretting. But in my heart there was never any question. In my heart I knew he was the man for me, table manners or no. And where love is concerned, it's our heart that matters most." She glanced down. "What about you, Sister? What does your heart tell you about Brother King?"

Lou didn't even need to consider her answer. "It tells me he's the one for me. That as long as I live, there will never be another. That without him I'm an empty shell."

Tamar's green eyes were twinkling. "So much for your doubts, eh?"

Lou thought about their discussion the remainder of

the day. That evening she sat with Zach instead of with the women, her head on his shoulder, savoring the sweet warmth of being devotedly in love. Nothing could spoil that moment. Or so she thought until he turned to her with features as grave as a cemetery.

"We've got trouble brewing."

Chapter Seven

Late that afternoon Zach had been roving well to the north of the wagon train, beyond the Platte. He was returning, about to recross the river, when he came on tracks left by four horses in soft earth.

The riders had dismounted to drink, their moccasin prints as clear as day. Prints that told Zach a lot.

No two tribes fashioned their footwear exactly the same. The shapes of the soles, the stitching patterns employed, and other details were different. Anyone versed in the varied styles could immediately tell which tribe the owner of any given moccasins belonged to.

In this case Zach recognized the quartet as Nadowessioux, as the voyageurs of old called them. Or, as they were more commonly called in recent times, the Sioux. Other tribes referred to them as the Lakotas. Misleading names, since the Sioux were made up of half a dozen branches, or subtribes, who called themselves Minniconjous, or Brules, or Oglalas, or Sans Arcs, among others.

All were fierce fighters. Their men lived for war, for counting coup and renown in battle in order to rise high in the councils of their people. Among their most bitter enemies were the Blackfeet, who had been trying for decades to drive the Sioux out, without success.

To say the Sioux weren't fond of whites was an understatement. They didn't like how more and more white men came west each year. They didn't like how the whites crossed their territory as the whites saw fit and slaughtered their game without any thought to how it would affect the Sioux. Consequently, wagon trains had been reporting trouble with the Sioux with increasing frequency.

So far there was little the whites could do except complain to a government that turned a deaf ear. The Army, largely confined to maneuvers east of the Mississippi, was next to useless.

When trains were raided they were on their own. Which accounted for why so many included a hundred wagons or better. The theory was that the more men, the more guns, and the more guns, the less likely the Sioux were to try anything.

The pilgrims from Ohio had erred greatly in having such a small party. Their train was puny, ripe pickings for seasoned warriors.

Zach's greatest fear was that the Sioux would discover his charges. He'd spent every available minute since entering their domain off scouting, on the lookout for precisely what he had found.

The four warriors weren't enough to constitute a war party. More than likely they were hunters, out after food. A clue that a Sioux village must be close by, no more than a day or two away.

Zach hadn't mentioned his discovery to the whites. What good would it do to put the women and children in a panic? But he couldn't keep the news from Lou, and now, as he finished, he could tell she didn't regard it as ominously as he did.

"You say the tracks led off in the other direction? To the northwest?"

"Yes."

"Then we have nothing to worry about. The warriors have no idea we're here. We're safe enough."

"For how long?"

Snickering, Louisa placed her hands on his. "Leave it to you to look at the bright side."

"You shouldn't poke fun," Zach said. "Twelve white men don't stand a prayer against hundreds of Sioux. This whole train would be wiped out."

"Maybe we should veer to the south," Lou suggested.

"And lose our daily source of water?" Zach had given the idea considerable thought but decided the disadvantages outweighed the merits.

"Only a couple of miles or so. At night we'll move back in close enough to water the stock."

"It would delay us even more. And being caught out on the prairie would be worse than being caught near the river where there's cover and plenty to drink."

"Then we're doing the best we can under the circumstances. Quit giving yourself an ulcer." Lou kissed him on the tip of his nose. "My grandfather had one and it pretty near killed him."

Zach made sure no one was paying any attention to them, then said, "I'd like you to come along tomorrow and help me scout. The two of us can cover a lot more ground than I can by myself."

"I'm flattered," Lou said.

Zach added a stipulation: "Just so long as you're never out of my sight."

"I *was* flattered."

Zach was sorry she was miffed, but it couldn't be helped. She had no inkling of how deadly the Sioux were. He did, though. A few years ago, his family had barely escaped with their lives after a clash with the Oglalas. "It's safer that way. You know it as well as I do."

Lou wasn't so sure their mutual safety was his main concern. She suspected he wanted her close to him to keep an eye on her. Which annoyed her no end. She hated being treated like a simpleton. But she swallowed her pride, replying, "Whatever you think is best."

The sun was a glorious crown heralding the advent of a new day when Zachary King and Louisa May Clark spurred their rested mounts on ahead of the lumbering Conestogas. For a while they stuck with the winding Platte, Zach checking constantly for sign of the Sioux on the south shore. At a convenient gravel bar they crossed to the north side and rode westward, spreading out, Lou by the river and Zach off on the plain.

By midmorning Zach was beginning to think Lou was right and he had been upset over nothing. The only spore he found was that of buffalo, deer, and smaller animals.

Toward noon Zach reined the bay toward the waterway. He hadn't been paying much attention to Lou and was troubled to note she wasn't where he thought she should be. Rising in the stirrups, he saw her farther back, on a knee by the water. Slaking her thirst, he assumed, and trotted over.

"What do you make of this?" Lou asked, nodding at a tract of mud.

Zach slid down and hunkered. A lone Lakota warrior had stood at that very spot less than an hour before. The man had squatted, possibly to drink, then headed across the Platte. The only prints were the warrior's. "Where's his horse?"

"I was wondering the same thing."

Zach straightened. Sioux never went anywhere on foot. As soon as they were old enough to be thrown on a horse, they were taught to ride. Horses were part and parcel of their existence, a symbol of prowess as well as wealth. For a warrior to be without one was extraordinary.

"Maybe his animal gave out on him," Lou opined.

"In that case he should be heading back to his village," Zach responded, "which is somewhere north of the river, not the direction he's going."

Lou walked to her mare and raised her foot to a stirrup. "We should go after him."

"One of us should," Zach agreed. "The other should backtrack a short ways. Maybe we'll find the answer."

Lou's saddle creaked as she straddled it. "Let me guess which one you want me to do." She swung the mare around. "I'll backtrack for a mile or so, then catch up with you."

"Be careful."

"Always."

Zach was glad she hadn't argued. Remounting, he forded the Platte, which rose only a couple of feet at that point, and dogged the Lakota southward.

The man seemed to have a definite goal, judging by how his tracks bore in a straight line. His stride showed he wasn't in any hurry.

Taking his own sweet time to avoid detection, Zach paused frequently to scan the waving ocean of grass. He estimated the settlers were two to three miles to the east, so the mystery warrior posed no threat to them.

A considerable distance had been covered when Zach spied a stick figure in the distance. He immediately dismounted and resorted to a trick he had seen Comanches use, a trick he liked so much, he had taught it to the bay. Gripping the bridle, Zach pulled downward while simultaneously slapping his free hand against the bay's right foreleg. The horse, snorting, carefully lowered onto its side.

"Well done," Zach said, patting the animal's neck. Now the Sioux couldn't spot it—if he hadn't already done so.

Tucking at the waist, Zach angled toward the stick figure. The warrior was moving back and forth as if searching for something. What it could be, Zach couldn't guess.

A slow, silent stalk was called for. Zach stayed low,

peeking above the grass now and again to make sure the Sioux wasn't coming toward him. To get close enough to see the man's features took a quarter of an hour. When at last Zach could, he breathed a little easier.

The Sioux was elderly, his long hair as gray as that of a gray fox, his face as wrinkled as a dried-out apple. He was slim of build, almost frail, and the only weapon he carried was a knife in a sheath on his left hip. Over his right shoulder hung a beaded parfleche.

As Zach looked on, the man squatted, drew the knife, and pried at a small flower of a type Zach was unfamiliar with. Once the plant was dug out, the Sioux examined its roots, then placed the entire plant in the parfleche.

To the settlers, what the old man was doing would make no sense. To Zach it spoke volumes. The Sioux was a healer, or shaman, as the whites liked to brand them, and was gathering plants to use as medicine.

Whites tended to belittle Indian remedies, but Zach had been cured by his mother's too many times to doubt their effectiveness. Indians relied on a wide variety of tinctures, ointments, and balms, the Shoshones included. They had cures for everything from stomach gas to poison, and many of their medicines were derived from common plants. Raw honeysuckle roots, for example, were pounded and applied to swellings and sores. Sagebrush leaves were chewed to soothe indigestion. Boiled elderberry roots were helpful against inflammation.

The old man rose. He moved rather stiffly, resuming his hunt, and leading Zach to think the plants might be for the man himself. Zach knew a Shoshone of comparable age whose joints forever ached, and who depended on daily doses of juniper tea, or *paal*, as the Shoshones called it, to get around.

Flat on his belly, Zach snaked closer, more out of curiosity than anything else. Now that he had established that the Sioux posed no threat, he had no real reason to stay. That is, until a troubling thought occurred to him.

For the old warrior to be so lightly armed was extremely unusual. Even when only out gathering medicine, weapons were called for. A bow or war club, at the very least. Yet the healer had neither.

Nor did he have a mount.

The first fact indicated that the Sioux deemed the vicinity fairly safe. The second indicated the oldster couldn't have come very far. Maybe he had a camp on the north side of the river—or maybe he had a *lodge*.

And where there was one lodge, there were invariably more.

Zach wanted to slap himself for not realizing the truth sooner. The oldster had no horse and was so lightly armed because he was near a village. A village located somewhere north-northwest of the Platte.

A village toward which Lou was unwittingly riding at that very moment.

Zach almost leaped up to run back to the bay. He had to get to Lou, had to verify she was safe. But when he glanced again at the old warrior, he was surprised to find the man had halted and was gazing in his direction. Worried he had somehow given himself away, Zach froze.

The Sioux showed no fear, no apprehension. His hands were folded in front of him, his posture relaxed.

Zach waited for the man to do or say something, but he was like a statue. Debating whether to crawl off, Zach's pulse quickened at a sound from behind him. He mistook it for a footstep. But then it was repeated, the dull *thump* of a heavy hoof, and he twisted his head, knowing what he would see before he saw it.

The bay had learned how to lie down on command, but it wasn't very good at *staying* down. It had grown tired of waiting and traipsed after him. Only ten feet away, it stopped and stared, awaiting its master.

Zach looked toward the old Sioux. The man, smiling, said something in the Sioux tongue. Unwilling to expose himself, Zach racked his brain for a way out of his predicament.

The healer's hands flowed in sign language. "I called Mole."

He was addlepated, Zach figured, and had signed to the bay. But the next movement of the Sioux's fingers hinted he was more alert and much more clever than Zach had given him credit for being.

"You no hide. I no hurt."

The man knew he was there! Zach slowly rose, the Hawken at his side. By rights he should shoot the man dead; the Sioux and Shoshones were long-standing enemies. But he couldn't bring himself to slay someone who was defenseless.

"Question. You called?" Mole signed.

Leaning the Hawken against his leg, Zach replied, "I called Stalking Coyote. I Shoshone warrior."

One of the Sioux's eyebrows arched. "You no look Shoshone."

"My father white man," Zach explained. Now that he had been caught he was eager to leave, to find Louisa.

Alarm etched Mole. "Question. White men near?"

"No," Zach signed, but it was obvious the oldster didn't believe him. Just as it was obvious what Mole would do as soon as he was gone: return to the Sioux village and alert them. War parties would be sent out. It wouldn't take long to locate the wagon train, and the prairie would flow red. Zach leveled the Hawken.

Mole recoiled, then signed, "Question. You kill me?"

Zach didn't respond. What choice did he have? It was the life of one man weighed in the balance against the lives of fifty-two others.

"Why?" Mole asked.

The Sioux deserved to know that much. Cradling the rifle, Zach signed, "You tell your people. They hurt whites."

"Question. Whites hurt us?"

"No. Whites go mountains," Zach disclosed.

"Why?"

Zach made a fist of his right hand, a bit below his

right shoulder, then dipped the fist a few inches. It was the sign for "sit" or "remain," the equivalent of saying the whites were going to the Rockies to live.

The news shocked Mole. "Whites sit in mountains all time?"

"All future. Yes," Zach said.

Mole digested the information before responding. "Question. They live Shoshone land?"

"No. Ute country."

Mole grinned. "You speak two tongues."

The man was calling him a lair, accusing him of making the whole thing up. "I speak straight tongue," Zach insisted.

"Utes happy whites come?"

"Utes not know."

At this Mole laughed heartily. "Utes find out, Utes maybe kill whites."

"Maybe," Zach signed.

"Whites know Utes maybe kill?"

"Yes."

Mole laughed some more. "Whites fools. Stay own country better."

The man would get no argument there, not when Zach was of the same opinion.

"Question. Whites no live Oglala country?"

"No. Whites cross Oglala country."

Mole seemed to reach a decision and squared his slim shoulders. "Question. We make peace?"

He was offering to strike a deal. "My ears open," Zach signed. His way of saying he was willing to listen to what the Sioux had in mind.

"You no kill Mole. Mole no tell people whites cross Oglala country."

Trust. It boiled down to trust. Could Zach rely on the oldster to do as he promised, or would Mole break his vow and rush home to spread word of the invaders?

Zach couldn't predict which it would be. The smart thing was to shoot Mole, sealing his lips and safeguarding the settlers in one fell swoop. But although Zach girded himself, he couldn't squeeze the trigger.

"What you think?" the old man urged. "Yes? No?"

"Yes," Zach signed, hoping against hope he hadn't sent fifty-two people to an early end.

Lowering his chin to his chest as if in a token of respect, Mole turned and continued searching for plants.

Zach stepped to the bay but hesitated. Part of him still wanted to shoot the Sioux.

Mole, adjusting the parfleche, glanced at him. "Leave Oglala country fast, Stalking Coyote."

"Fast we can," Zach signed.

"Tomorrow, next day maybe, many warriors hunt buffalo," Mole revealed. "Many warriors ride prairie."

Zach showed his gratitude for the warning by signing, "Thank you. You good man."

"I old man," Mole signed. "I see enough blood."

Further delay invited disaster. Quickly forking the saddle, Zach reined around and galloped toward the Platte. Before too long, in a tremendous spray of water, he hastened across and soon picked up Louisa's trail. The mare's tracks guided him to the northwest.

If anything had happened to her!—the thought was too horrible for Zach to finish. He was the one who had sent her north, so whatever befell her was his fault. In seeking to protect her from harm, he had done the exact opposite and sent her into the bear's den, as it were.

Within a mile the terrain changed from monotonous flatland to a series of hillocks. As barren as could be, they afforded no cover whatsoever. Yet Lou had gone in among them rather than around, sticking to the old Sioux's trail as Zach instructed her.

The hillocks resembled waves on an ocean, rolling one after the other off into the midday haze. On none was a rider visible.

Zach raced up one slope and down another, always praying to spot Lou over the next crest, always disappointed when he didn't. Then, seething with frustration, he trotted up yet another and beheld the mare below, grazing with its reins dangling.

Acting on the assumption that Lou must be close at hand, Zach brought the bay to a stop next to the mare, hopped off, and climbed the next slope, mindful he didn't show himself when he reached the top.

Flattening, Zach crawled the final three feet and poked his head high enough to see what lay beyond. Suddenly icy fingers encased his heart. His grip on the rifle tightened to where his knuckles were white.

"No!" he breathed. "It can't be!"

But it was.

Zach had found the Sioux village. And being led into it, surrounded by a score of Oglalas, her arms in the grasp of a brawny warrior, was the woman Zach loved more than life itself.

Of all the dumb things Louisa May Clark had ever done, she rated her capture as one of the dumbest.

She'd had no problem backtracking the Sioux, but had about despaired of ever reaching the man's camp when the merry tinkle of voices fell on her ears. Slowing, Lou reined up in a hollow and advanced on foot. The voices were speaking in a language she couldn't recollect ever hearing, and which she took for granted must be the Sioux tongue. Mingled with the voices were high-pitched squeals of children and the feminine laughter.

Louisa didn't know what to make of it. What were women and kids doing in the middle of nowhere? Dropping onto her hands and knees, she peeked over the rim.

Before her marveling gaze unfolded a large Sioux village, lodge after lodge after lodge, covering acre after acre. Constructed of buffalo hides and long poles, the majority bore painted symbols of some sort. Horses milled in herds, hundreds of them, enough to outfit an army. Sioux were everywhere, the women skinning hides, drying strips of meat on wood frames, sewing, gossiping, and playing games, the men talking in groups or sharpening knives or cleaning guns, the children running and yelling and behaving as children everywhere generally behaved.

Lou had to get out of there before she was spotted. She started to slide back down from the rim, then paused. At the base of the hillock she was on were the women and children she had heard squealing and laughing, involved in a game that consisted of pushing a wooden hoop. There seemed to be five to a side, with the object being for one side to steal the hoop from the other by spearing it with sticks. They were having a grand old time, chortling and cackling in gay abandon. Lou watched a minute, then turned to depart.

Several yards away stood a small boy attired in a short breechclout smeared with grime. His mouth agape, he appeared as flabbergasted as Lou. Thinking swiftly, Lou smiled to show she was friendly.

The boy backed up a step, his lips working but no sound coming out.

Sensing what he would do next, Lou pushed upright and ran. But she failed to take the loose clods dotting the slope into account, and just as the boy let out with a shriek that would do justice to a banshee, her left foot slipped out from under her and she crashed onto her back. Her rifle went flying. In a choking cloud of dust, she started sliding.

The boy's shrieks rang in her ears as Lou desperately sought to stop and stand. But the steep incline and gravity were impossible to resist. She gouged her elbows into the soil, she clawed at the ground, she jammed her heels in—to no avail. Amid a rain of pebbles and dirt, she slid clear to the bottom and came to rest on her side, caked with dust but essentially unhurt except for a few scrapes and bruises.

Lou rose, scanning the slope for the Hawken. The boy was still screeching, and from the far side rose answering yells. It wouldn't be long before the women and the rest of the children came rushing to see what had him so agitated, but Lou wasn't leaving without her rifle. She sprinted back up to claim it.

The boy stopped his caterwauling, only to shout the same single word over and over again, pointing at her each time he did.

Another couple of steps and the Hawken would be close enough to grab. Lou saw a shadow move across it and she looked up, into the hawkish visage of a stout warrior with a barrel chest. Where he had come from she had no idea.

The next instant the Sioux leaped, tackling her so hard the breath whooshed from her lungs.

Lou made an effort to grab a pistol but arms thick with corded muscle seized her wrists and wrenched them behind her. Her captor was immensely strong, and he hoisted her erect with ease. Agony lanced her shoulders, her elbows, as she was hauled to the top of the hill.

The women and children who had been playing the hoop game were being joined by a swiftly gathering crowd. They regarded Lou coldly as the warrior propelled her down the other side—toward captivity or death.

Chapter Eight

Zach King's first impulse was to rush over the rise to her rescue. Common sense, and eight mounted warriors who trotted into view, kept him where he was. The warriors made for the group encircling Louisa.

The man who was holding her addressed them, then pointed at the hill Zach was on.

Zach turned and ran. They were after her horse or else intended to backtrack her to see if other whites were nearby. He almost tripped flying down the slope but recovered. Two more bounds brought him to the animals. Vaulting onto the bay, he reined it close to the mare, snagged her reins, and galloped to the left, going around the next hillock rather than up and over it.

It tore Zach apart to leave Lou behind. Icy claws were slicing his heart to ribbons. Yet it couldn't be helped. He had to escape so he could return later and spirit her to safety. Freeing her wouldn't be easy, not with an entire village to contend with, but if it was humanly possible he would succeed or die trying.

Once he was at the end of the hillock, Zach smacked

his legs against the bay and sped southward. He had four, maybe five minutes before the warriors lit out after him. They'd find where the bay and mare had been and streak in pursuit, eager to count coup.

In all the vast plains—in the entire length and breadth of the midcontinent mountains—no warriors were more courageous, none more filled with a fiery zest for combat than the Sioux. Whether it was the Oglalas, the Sans Arcs, the Minneconjous, or the Brules, they were a warrior people.

The measure of a tribe's fighting prowess was reflected in the sincere respect of their enemies. And in that regard, the ferocity of the Sioux had earned them the highest respect of powerful tribes like the Shoshones, the Blackfeet, and the Cheyenne.

Only lately was the white man learning how truly formidable they were. Zach's pa was of the opinion that in the years ahead, as more whites flocked west, bloody clashes would grow more frequent, resulting in open war. It was inevitable, his father said, because the whites would never be content with the land east of the Mississippi and the Sioux would never willingly give theirs up.

Zach had gone past two more hillocks. Cutting to the left, he rode between the next two to reduce the chance of the Sioux catching sight of him. Inciting their bloodlust would give them incentive to overtake him that much more quickly.

At the end of the hill Zach galloped south again, his goal the river and the thick vegetation bordering it, the only decent cover for miles around. But he couldn't go anywhere near the wagon train; the Sioux mustn't learn about the settlers or the pilgrims were doomed.

Every yard he covered worsened Zach's emotional turmoil. He tried not to think of Lou, tried not to dwell on what the Sioux might be doing to her. He had to keep reminding himself it was unlikely they'd harm her. In most instances involving female captives it was customary for a warrior to take the captive as a wife. And that wouldn't happen anytime soon to Lou. A council would be held. The tribal leaders would discuss what to do about her. So Lou was safe enough for a while.

Still, Zach couldn't help but worry. Louisa was everything to him—his very breath given flesh, his very soul made real. He loved her with all he was, and he couldn't bear the idea of being separated.

When Zach was younger, he'd never given much thought to marriage beyond a vague notion that one day he'd like to be like his pa and have a wife and family. To his way of thinking, the woman didn't exist who could win his undying devotion. Yet the moment he set eyes on Lou, he was hopelessly lost. There was something about her, a special quality that something deep inside of him responded to. Two hearts entwined, Lou liked to call it. Soul mates.

Years earlier, Zach and his mother had gone for a summer's stroll, picking flowers to put in a vase. At one point he'd asked her why she had married his pa. Why, of all the men in the world, she had picked Nate King. His mother had looked at him in that wise way she had and smiled. "Because I knew he was the one for me. There could be no other. He made me complete."

At the time, Zach hadn't fully understood. But now he did. Lou did the same to him. She completed him. They were two halves of a coin, as different as night and day, yet they blended as seamlessly together as dawn and dusk.

Zach had given himself to her totally. She would be his wife, the mother of his children, the woman he would spend the rest of his days with. And no one, *no one*, was going to take her away from him. He hadn't let the Blackfeet do it. He hadn't let her own relatives do it. And he would damned if he'd let the Sioux do it, either.

Zach felt his eyes begin to moisten. He grit his teeth, refusing to be weak. To fuel his anger, he imagined what he would do to the Sioux if they so much as laid a finger on her.

It had been months since Zach counted coup on an enemy, months since he gave counting coup any thought at all. Yet before he met Lou, it had been all he thought about. His utmost desire back then had been to rise in the ranks of the Shoshone nation, to become a leader, a chief, by counting more coup than anyone else. It was a dream most every Shoshone boy shared.

Then Lou came into his life. Instead of idling the hours away daydreaming about victories in bloody battles, he had taken to daydreaming about the two of them in intimate embrace, to envisioning having a cabin of their own and playful tykes to fill the cabin with laughter and joy.

Zach hadn't realized it until that moment, but he no longer hankered to be a great war chief. He would be content with Lou and a family.

Strange how he had turned out more like his pa than he'd ever anticipated he would.

Nate King could have been a prominent man in the Shoshone nation. Long ago the tribe had formally adopted him, and the Shoshones considered him one of their own. He'd had the opportunity to rise to a position of leadership to rival that of Touch the Clouds, but he had been content to live the life of a trapper—a decision Zach had always secretly seen as a mistake. Now, though, the shoe was on the other foot, as the saying went, and Zach craved the exact same thing his father had: the love of a good woman, and a loving family to provide for.

Now his dream was in jeopardy. The good woman who had claimed his heart was in peril. All the plans they had made for their future together were on the brink of ruin. Come what may, he must save her. All he had to do was elude the Sioux until nightfall.

Savage whoops testified that it would be easier contemplated than done. Twisting, Zach spied the warriors sweeping in a knot into the open. Baying like bloodhounds, they bore down on him.

Louisa May Clark stood straight and proud, refusing to show any fear, any trepidation. Fully fifty Sioux surrounded her, with more arriving every second. Her wrists had been bound behind her back, and she stood in front of a high lodge into which the warrior who captured her had disappeared.

Other warriors were present, but they stood aloof, studying her. The women and children, however, were less restrained. They poked her, they prodded her, they plucked at her clothes and pulled on her hair.

No one had relieved Lou yet of her ammo pouch or powder horn. Her pistols and knife were gone, though, taken into the lodge by her stout captor.

Lou knew that a bunch of men had ridden off, presumably to fetch her mare, and she was surprised they hadn't returned. She prayed Zach wouldn't come after her, but if he did, that he wasn't caught. He was her only hope of rescue. The odds seemed preposterous, one man against an entire village, but she had unbounded faith in him.

A heavyset woman approached, using a cane for support. Inherently cruel features creased in contempt as she jabbed the cane into Lou's ribs and made comments that brought smiles to many of the onlookers.

Lou had heard tales, horrible tales, of the atrocities committed by various tribes, and she braced herself for the worst. Zach had told her that if she was ever taken captive, a willing warrior might take a fancy to her and make her his mate. But she couldn't count on that. Not given how plain she was. She'd mentioned as much to Zach and upset him greatly.

Lou was tickled no end that her sweetheart thought she was beauty incarnate, but the simple truth was that she was as ordinary as bread. Her body was too slender, her bosom barely big enough to distinguish her from a male, her lips and cheeks much too thin.

In Lou's estimation she was one step removed from a goat, so it wouldn't surprise her at all if there wasn't a warrior in the whole village attracted enough to claim her.

That left two alternatives. One, they'd kill her outright. Female or not, she was white, and that was enough to feed her to the worms. Or, two, she'd become their slave, forced to work from dawn to dusk doing every menial job under the sun.

Abruptly, the flap parted and out strode the warrior who had captured her. He wasn't alone. Two others, whose bearing marked them as leaders, regarded her with keen interest, one going so far as to squeeze her limbs and belly as if she were a calf he was sizing up for slaughter.

"Keep your hands to yourself, why don't you?" Lou complained, well aware that her request was so much gibberish to them.

The heavyset woman poked her again, more forcefully, and uttered a remark that could only be construed as a threat. She glared at Lou, and Lou, not to be cowed, glared back.

The three warriors moved to one side and spoke quietly, determining her fate. Lou watched them closely for a clue as to what they were thinking, but their expressions gave little away.

The woman with the cane poked her again, for no reason whatsoever. Angry, Lou lashed out, kicking at the cane. She didn't intend to hurt the woman, only to show displeasure at how she was being treated. But suddenly one of the warriors was there, his brawny arm rising. Lou was backhanded across the cheek. She stumbled against the onlookers but stayed on her feet. As she was pushed back, she tasted the salty tang of her own blood.

The tall man who had struck her raised his hand to

do so again but desisted at a word from one of the others, who now came up to Lou and spoke to her in the Sioux tongue.

Lou shook her head, saying, "I wish to blazes I knew what you're saying." She entertained the hope that someone in the village might know English, as had one of the Pawnees, but no one stepped forward to translate.

She shouldn't be surprised, Lou told herself. The Pawnees had come into contact with whites long before the Sioux and had befriended them, whereas the Sioux only wanted to wipe the whites out.

The tall man turned to the woman with the cane and they had a curt exchange, after which the heavyset woman smacked her cane against Lou's shin, then motioned.

The Sioux parted, permitting Lou to move in the direction the crone wanted. She held her head up and walked as if she were marching in a parade, refusing to show them the slightest hint of defeat. A few of the adults grinned at her bravado. Most, though, regarded her with distrust and not a little dislike.

At a lodge on the east side of the village, Lou was brought to a halt by a blow to the shoulder blades.

Walking to the flap, the heavyset woman opened it and motioned for Lou to precede her.

To balk would only earn Lou another blow from the cane. Ducking, she entered and automatically moved to the left, as was required.

Few whites back east had any inkling of the proper conduct expected of anyone who entered an Indian dwelling. Tepee etiquette varied a bit from tribe to tribe, as did every other aspect of Indian society, but by and large the basic rules were simple: No one should enter if the flap was down as that was a sign the occupants did not want to be disturbed, but if the flap was open visitors were allowed to go right in. Men always bore to the right, women to the left. No one must ever walk between the fire and whoever else might be inside, as that was rated the worst of medicine. Men could sit cross-legged, women could not. Any woman who did was considered shameless. Women either perched on their heels or with their legs curled under them to preserve their modesty.

Zach had made a special effort to verse Lou in lodge etiquette for when they visited the Shoshones next summer. So after moving to the left, she sank down with her legs curled, as was required. But she hadn't roosted two seconds when the heavyset woman was above her, hitting her on the shoulders and shrilly berating her.

Lou stood, confused, not knowing what she had done wrong. The woman pointed at a partially skinned rabbit lying beside a knife and at a battered iron pot.

"You want me to finish butchering your supper for you, is that it?" Lou asked.

The woman pointed again and spoke testily.

"How am I supposed to do it with my hands tied?" Lou asked, and wagged her arms to stress her point.

Grunting, the woman bent, picked up the knife, and twirled it to signal Lou to turn around. A stroke of the razor-edged blade was all it took to part the strands like so much flax. Then the woman shoved the hilt into Lou's hand and turned away.

Lou hefted the knife and glanced at the flap, which the woman had left open. She could reach it and slip outside before the woman was the wiser. With so many horses in the village, finding a mount wouldn't pose a problem. But escaping on it would. Scores of Sioux were abroad at any given minute, and they would raise a hue and cry that would result in her swift recapture.

For now, Lou reflected, it was better to play along, to do as she was instructed to do. Sooner or later a better opportunity would present itself. When it did, she must be ready to seize the moment.

Kneeling, Lou set to work on the rabbit. She chopped off the head, peeled off the hide, and quartered it. Dropping the chunks in the pot, she set the knife down and wiped her hands clean on her buckskins.

The heavyset woman had been cutting wild onions on a flat slab of rock. Now she rose, examined Lou's handiwork, and shoved the iron pot at her.

"You want it cut up some more?" Lou asked, uncertain of what was required.

Beckoning, the woman limped to the doorway and exited. Thirty yards to the east flowed a small stream. The woman pointed at it, then at Lou, then at the utensil.

"I get it," Lou said. "You want me to fill the pot with water." She was amazed when the woman went back inside, leaving her on her own. A quick survey sufficed to show that no other Sioux were in the immediate vicinity.

Lou headed for the stream along a well-worn footpath, grinning at how ridiculously easy they had made it. She would head across the prairie and lose herself in the high grass. Later she would bear to the south to intercept the wagon train. As slowly as the Conestogas moved, she'd overtake them in no time.

Lou was looking over her shoulder to make sure no one was keeping track of her when a startled exclamation enabled her to stop before she bumped into a pair of women coming the other direction.

"Sorry," Lou blurted, stepping aside.

Appraising her as if she were a rattler about to strike, the pair gave her a wide berth, staring until they reached the lodges.

Lou sought to make light of the situation. "Now I know how a fish in a fish bowl feels." Hastening on, she came to the stream that was no wider than a narrow country lane and no deeper than the pot she was holding. About to drop it and cross over, she whirled when murmuring voices alerted her she wasn't alone.

Far from it.

A dozen or more women were lined along the water's edge, some washing clothes, one filling a water skin, others resting with their feet in the stream.

Lou rarely swore, but she did so now. Foiled, she hunkered and filled the pot, taking her time so she could gauge her chances of fleeing. Her inevitable conclusion was that it would be pointless to try, and would only rile the Sioux.

One of the younger women was smiling at her, so Lou returned the favor. She could use all the friends she could make. But the woman promptly averted her face as if shy or embarrassed.

"Talk about being popular," Lou jested.

Having done as she was supposed to, Lou stood and longingly scanned the plain. Freedom was so close, so very close, yet she might as well have to reach the moon for all the good it did her. Sighing, she held the pot against her waist so as not to spill it and ambled back.

Several women passed her along the way. They, too, avoided her as if she were infected with the plague.

At the end of the trail, waiting with his arms folded across his chest, was the same tall warrior who had directed the heavyset woman to take Lou to the lodge. Lou had the impression he had been watching her all along, and she was glad, now, that she hadn't tried to run off. Deliberately not looking at him, she walked on by and into the tepee.

The heavyset woman had a small fire going. She impatiently gestured for Lou to give her the pot, then hung it on a tripod over the crackling flames.

Lou moved to the left and sat, awaiting the next development. She didn't wait long. Through the opening came the tall warrior, who took a seat toward the rear, on the other side of the fire, the traditional seat of the owner of the lodge.

It put everything in a whole new, worrisome light. For if this was his lodge, then he had Lou brought to it for a specific purpose.

He was going to make her his wife!

* * *

Over half a mile had been covered at breakneck speed. Zach was still ahead. But the big bay, which he'd pushed so hard earlier, was beginning to flag, while the Sioux were coming on strong, whopping and hollering, confident they would soon overtake him. And they just might.

Zach had the mare's reins looped around his left wrist so he wouldn't lose her. She was keeping up easily, since she wasn't the least bit tired. Glancing at her gave him an idea, inspired by a trick he'd once witnessed a wily Comanche use.

Shifting in the saddle, Zach saw that his pursuers were several hundred yards behind. They whooped louder, waving lances and bows.

Facing front, Zach slid his moccasins out of the stirrups. He tugged on the mare's reins to bring her a little closer, then hiked his legs, bent them at the knees, and braced them on the bay's broad back. Another few strides to adjust to the rolling rhythm, then Zach launched himself into the air, sideways, leaping from the bay onto the mare, a reckless, dangerous gambit that nearly cost him his life. As he alighted, he slipped and would have pitched over the mare's shoulder had he not seized hold of her flying mane.

In another second Zach's feet were in the mare's stirrups and he flew onto the south. Only now he was astride a fresh mount, the bay's reins wrapped around his other hand.

Angry yells from the Sioux showed what they thought of his tactic.

Zach began to gain ground, a little at first but more as the minutes crawled by. The Sioux mounts, already quirted to their limit, were tiring.

A line of vegetation appeared, the belt bordering the Platte, Zach's only hope of eluding the Oglalas. He had a seven-hundred-yard lead when he reached a fringe of cottonwoods. Plunging in, he slowed and veered to the right. To go the other way would lead the Sioux straight to the wagon train.

Threading through the growth, Zach rode to the river—and on into it. Keeping to the center where the water was deepest, he forged westward. Ordinarily the ruse would be enough to wash away all trace of his passage, but the Platte was so shallow, so sluggish, that the Sioux would still be able to trail him. The muddy water would be a dead giveaway.

After a couple of hundred feet, Zach brought the horses to shore and went even faster. He had no set plan beyond escaping and later circling wide to return to the village shortly after dark.

The settlers deserved to be warned that they were near an encampment of hostiles, but Zach couldn't very well do it with the Sioux on his tail. He'd warn them later, after Lou was safe. In the meantime, if the Sioux stumbled on the train, the whites would have to get by on their own.

Zach couldn't help it that circumstances had conspired against him. So what if the whites wouldn't stand a prayer against the Oglalas? He had done all he could. And Lou's welfare mattered more to him than theirs. She came first. She always came first.

However, much to Zach's annoyance, he couldn't stop thinking of all those women and children, couldn't stop thinking of their fate should they fall into the Oglalas' clutches. His conscience pricked at him. Was it right to hold fifty-two lives in the balance against the life of a single person?

"It can't be helped!" Zach said aloud. But he was deluding no one but himself, and he knew it.

After traveling another half a mile, Zach came to a stop and checked his back trail. There was no sign of the Sioux, but they were bound to be along shortly. Going around the next bend, he reined up, dismounted, and tied the horses to an oak.

Hurrying back to the bend, Zach eased down into a cleft in the bank. It was just wide enough and deep enough to provide the cover he needed. Resting the

Join the Western Book Club
and GET 4 FREE* BOOKS NOW!
A $19.96 VALUE!

Yes! I want to subscribe to the Western Book Club.

Please send me my **4 FREE* BOOKS**. I have enclosed $2.00 for shipping/handling. Each month I'll receive the four newest Leisure Western selections to preview for 10 days. If I decide to keep them, I will pay the Special Members Only discounted price of just $3.36 each, a total of $13.44, plus $2.00 shipping/handling ($22.30 US in Canada). This is a **SAVINGS OF AT LEAST $6.00** off the bookstore price. There is no minimum number of books I must buy, and I may cancel the program at any time. In any case, the **4 FREE* BOOKS** are mine to keep.

*In Canada, add $5.00 shipping/handling per order for the first shipment. For all future shipments to Canada, the cost of membership is $22.30 US, which includes shipping and handling. (All payments must be made in US dollars.)

NAME: ______________________

ADDRESS: ______________________

CITY: ______________ **STATE:** __________

COUNTRY: ______________ **ZIP:** __________

TELEPHONE: ______________________

E-MAIL: ______________________

SIGNATURE: ______________________

If under 18, Parent or Guardian must sign. Terms, prices, and conditions subject to change. Subscription subject to acceptance. Dorchester Publishing reserves the right to reject any order or cancel any subscription.

Hawken on the lip, he flexed and unflexed his fingers to limber them up for what was to come.

Zach was through running. To go on, to ride the horses into the ground, would sign not only his death warrant but Lou's, and that of all those with the train. Wisdom dictated he make a stand, that he try his best to discourage the Sioux, perhaps drive them off by slaying a few. The hitch was that the Oglalas might turn the tables and either capture or slay him.

The wait frayed his patience to the breaking point. Each second was an eternity. But at length Zach heard the thud of hoofs, the splash of water, and four warriors appeared.

Two of the Sioux were in the middle of the stream, and one was on either bank. The man on the north bank had his head bent to read the sign. The others were scouring the undergrowth. All four advanced slowly, warily, a lance cocked to hurl, arrows nocked to sinew strings.

Zach saw only the four. Evidently his pursuers had been unsure which direction he'd taken and split up, half going west, the rest east. So he had cut the odds dramatically. But the four heading east were bound to discover the wagon train. They'd relay the news to the village, and sometime tomorrow scores of painted Oglalas would spring an ambush on the unsuspecting whites.

Everything that could go wrong *was* going wrong. Lou's life was in peril, the settlers were at risk, and Zach himself might not live to greet the next dawn. Fate had boxed him in a corner, but Zach wasn't about to roll over and die.

The four warriors stopped. The man on the north bank was at the exact spot where Zach had paused, a short ways shy of the bend. The man made a comment that caused the other three to become even more wary. Then they advanced anew, moving abreast.

Zach knew that the instant he showed himself they would be on him like a pack of starving wolves on a bull elk. Placing a hand on each of his pistols, he willed himself to wait just a little longer, to let them get so close he couldn't possibly miss.

Another ten feet would do it.

Zach shut Lou from his mind. He shut the settlers from his thoughts. It was do-or-die time, as the mountain men were fond of saying.

He focused on the Sioux.

Then the warrior on the north bank spotted the Hawken and the top of Zach's head. Shouting to his companions, the man pointed at the cleft.

To a chorus of war whoops, the Sioux charged.

Chapter Nine

Louisa May Clark shifted her legs to relieve a cramp in her left calf. So intent was she on trying to figure out what was being said, she hadn't moved in the past ten minutes.

A quartet of older, distinguished warriors had arrived, one with braided gray hair that fell past his hips. They were having a parley with the tall warrior, and it was apparent she was the topic. Every so often, one nodded in her direction or pointed to her.

Lou wished she could understand. It would be nice to know if the tall warrior truly did have designs on her. If so, he was destined to be disappointed. Under no circumstances would Lou let him touch her. She hadn't saved herself for so long so her wedding night would be extra special only to be ravished against her will. Should he try, she'd claw his eyes, bite his throat, scratch him silly—in short, do everything she could to preserve her dignity.

As if he were privy to her thoughts, the tall warrior gave her a stern look. Lou didn't know what it meant.

The heavyset woman ignored the proceedings while busily mending a dress. All the warriors treated her as if she didn't exist, which Lou understood was fairly routine. In some tribes the females had little to say in how things were done. They were barred from councils and seldom became chiefs, their influence limited to the upkeep of lodges and the rearing of children.

Lou stiffened when the gray-haired warrior stood and came over to her. Squatting, he peered deep into her eyes, then addressed her at some length. He sounded kindly, even concerned, and it frustrated Lou keenly that she couldn't comprehend. Smiling, she made so bold as to place her hand on his forearm as a token of friendliness.

Sighing, the gray-haired warrior returned to the fire. The talk became almost as heated as the flames.

Lou wondered where Zach was, whether he had discovered her plight and what he would do once he had. Were she in his moccasins, she'd wait until dark and attempt to sneak into the village. But how would he find her amid so many lodges? Unless he'd been spying on the camp when she was brought in, he'd have no idea which tepee she was in.

The parley abruptly ended and the three distinguished warriors rose. Lou saw the gray-haired man give her a rather sad look as he departed. It didn't bode well.

The tall warrior snapped at the heavyset woman, who put down the dress she was mending and brought him a piece of jerked buffalo meat from a parfleche, one of several piled at the back. The woman helped herself to a piece but didn't offer any to their captive.

Lou felt her stomach growl. She refused to ask for any food, however. It would be a sign of weakness, of acceptance, and she would be damned if she would give in so meekly. The hungrier she was, the thirstier she became, the more it steeled her resolve to escape.

The tall warrior was staring at her again, thoughtfully.

Placing the jerky in his lap, he moved his hands in sign language. "Question. You called?"

Lou kept a blank face, pretending she didn't understand even though Zach had taught her the basics of sign, just enough to get by in a pinch when they visited the Shoshones. She didn't want the Sioux to find out, but she couldn't say exactly why. Maybe because she was afraid he'd ply her with questions about how she'd gotten there. Since it was unusual for whites to cross the plain in small parties, the tall Oglala might suspect she was with a wagon train and force her to reveal where it was. She couldn't let that happen. The settlers must be protected at all costs.

The tall warrior snorted in disgust, rose, and stepped in front of her. Before Lou could fathom what he was up to, he brusquely entwined his fingers in her hair and literally jerked her to her feet. She almost cried out, biting her lower lip to still her tongue.

Although Lou yearned to resist, she let him shove her to the flap and out the opening. His hand clamped onto the back of her neck as he forced her away from the lodge. Then he pointed to the south and gave her a quizzical look.

Lou was no dummy. He wanted to learn which direction she had come from. But she merely gestured helplessly.

The warrior's features clouded. He pointed to the southeast and again looked at her. This time when she gestured, he squeezed her neck, gouging his fingers into her flesh, and shook her as a grizzly might a doe.

Raw agony coursed through Lou from crown to toe, but she continued to play dumb. It earned her a poke that would have doubled her over were it not for the viselike hold on her neck.

Undeterred, the warrior tried a third time. He extended his arm to the southwest.

"Your mother was a polecat and your father a gutter rat," Lou said, smiling as sweetly as she was able. "I wouldn't tell you if you pulled my nails out one by one."

Disgust resurfaced, along with rising anger, and the warrior shook her once more, jarring her teeth and hurting her spine.

Still smiling, Lou said, "If I had a gun, you wouldn't be manhandling me, mister." He flung her bodily to the earth and she flung out her arms, landing on her hands and knees with bruising force.

His hands on his hips, the warrior walked completely around her, then hiked a foot as if to kick her. Apparently deciding she wasn't worth expending the energy, he lowered it again.

Lou didn't move, didn't speak, didn't do anything to make him madder than he already was. She remembered a story told by Winona King about several Shoshone maidens taken captive by a tribe whose name eluded her. Two of the maidens were later rescued by a Shoshone war party. In the interim the third had died, beaten to death when she'd sassed one of their captors.

Suddenly the warrior bent, grabbed Lou by the shoulders, and pushed her toward the flap. She entered without having to be told and returned to her proper place on the left side of the lodge. Lou thought the warrior would return, too, but his swarthy form didn't darken the entrance. Which suited her just fine.

The heavyset woman was stirring the stew with a tin spoon. Treating herself to a sip, she smacked her thick lips, smirking at Lou the whole while.

"Same to you," Lou said as her stomach rumbled. To take her mind off her hunger, she speculated on how it was that a tribe rumored to have no dealings with whites was able to acquire pots and spoons. Maybe they traded with other tribes who did have dealings. Or maybe—and a cold knot formed in her gut—maybe the utensils had been taken from wagon trains the Sioux raided.

Lou gazed at the top of the lodge, at the vent through which wisps of smoke were rising. How long before dark? She'd neglected to note the position of the sun when the warrior took her outside, and the vent would help her gauge when the sun went down.

There wasn't a lick of doubt whatsoever in Lou's mind that Zach would come for her. Her faith in him was as unbounded as her love. He would move mountains, as the saw went, to reach her. Nothing short of death would keep him from saving her, and since she refused to countenance the notion of him ever dying, her salvation was only hours away.

Lou didn't rate it the least bit strange that she had such limitless trust in him. Quite the contrary. Her trust seemed as natural as breathing, as ordinary as rain. That it had sprouted without any conscious deliberation on her part *was* remarkable, but then, so was love itself.

Love was the miracle of miracles, the greatest blessing any woman or man experienced in their mortal lifetime. It was also the great mystery of mysteries, for while poets had written about it for centuries and it had been celebrated in songs and sonnets since time immemorial, no one could say why it was that two people *fell* in love. What was it that made one man or woman so special? What unique quality made them stand out from the millions of other human beings on the planet?

Until Lou met Zach, she hadn't given much thought to such heady affairs. Fact was, she'd pretty much taken it for granted she'd never wed. Given her plain appearance and unexceptional personality, she'd assumed no man would ever find her interesting enough to want to spend the rest of his natural-born days with her.

It showed how much she knew.

Lou inadvertently giggled, eliciting a puzzled glance from the heavyset woman. "Ever felt true love?" Lou asked, knowing the Sioux wouldn't understand. "I have. And let me tell you, it's grand as grand can be."

The woman's puzzlement deepened, which amused Lou all the more. She giggled again, the mirth dying in her throat when a shadow filled the opening.

Into the lodge came the tall warrior. The heavyset

woman spoke, and he stopped and looked at Lou in displeasure.

What now? Lou wondered. Was it against Sioux custom to giggle?

Without warning, the warrior strode over and grabbed her by her hair. Lou, reacting in pure reflex, did the last thing she should have: She hit him.

The four warriors bore down on Zachary King like bronzed Furies, shrieking and brandishing weapons.

The man on the right let fly with a shaft that thudded into the soil inches from Zach's ear. Quick as thought, the Sioux notched another shaft and took swift aim.

A second man rose to hurl a lance as soon as he was within range.

The warrior on the north bank elevated a war club.

Only the top of Zach's head showed above the cleft. He hadn't moved since they spotted him, perhaps giving them the impression he was riveted in fear.

Nothing could have been further from the truth. Zach was allowing them to come closer, allowing them to get so close he couldn't possibly miss. Smoothbore pistols were most effective at short range, their penetration and stopping power enough to drop any man or beast at twenty paces.

Zach demonstrated as much when he exploded into action and flashed the flintlocks from under his belt. Straightening, he fired them both at the selfsame moment.

The bowman's chest was cored just as he unleashed a second arrow. He tumbled backward over his mount's rump, the arrow arcing off into the trees instead of into Zach's torso.

The warrior wielding the lance was violently wrenched around as a lead ball ripped into his cheek, shattering the bone. The ball drilled a bloody path through his cranium, shearing through tissue and more bone like a red-hot knife through wax, then burst out the rear of his skull, spraying gore and brains in all directions.

Dropping the pistols, Zach grabbed the Hawken. The other two were almost on top of him. One also had a lance; the other was the warrior with the war club. Since the lance posed the greater threat, Zach hastily fixed a bead and fired when its owner wasn't but ten feet off.

The shot lifted the Sioux clear off his horse to tumble end over end. With a sickening crunch, he crashed onto a cluster of small boulders.

That left the man on the north bank. Screeching in rage at the loss of his companions, he hurled himself from his animal, his war club aloft. As he descended, he brought it sweeping down.

Zach dived to the right, out the open end of the cleft, and landed in the stream. Heaving erect, he clutched at the Bowie as the Sioux came at him like an avenging Harpy. The club cleaved toward Zach's forehead, but he skipped backward, then evaded another savage swing and brought the Bowie to bear. But it hardly gave the Sioux pause. Snarling like a rabid coyote, the warrior swung again and again, always on the offensive, never giving Zach a moment to catch his breath.

Dodging, ducking, skipping to one side or the other, Zach spared himself from serious harm. But he couldn't maintain the frantic pace forever. Sooner or later, he'd make a mistake and the warrior would be on him with the speed of a striking viper.

It didn't help that a Bowie was no match for a war club, not when the latter was heavier and had a longer reach. Zach regretted not following his pa's advice to always carry a tomahawk as well as the big knife. A tomahawk was heftier, rendering it better able to withstand a club or other such weapon.

Sheer bloodlust contorted the warrior's features. His face was flushed, spittle dribbling over his lower lip and down his chin. Growling deep in his throat, he aimed a blow that would have crushed Zach's head like a rotten melon, but Zach pivoted on the heel of his left foot and avoided it, which only incensed the warrior more.

Zach's knife arm flashed. The Oglala had over-extended himself, and the sharp steel made him pay for his mistake by shearing deep, enough to scrape against the man's ribs.

Blood oozed as the Sioux stopped his rampaging assault and backed off several strides. He looked down at himself, touched his fingers to the wound, then raised his hand and smeared blood on both cheeks as an act of defiance.

Crouching, Zach waited for the next onslaught.

The warrior had learned his lesson. Rather than go berserk, he cautiously circled, the war club held poised to pound. He scrutinized Zach closely, taking his measure. Suddenly he swung, but it was a feint. He shifted in midswing and drove the club to the left, anticipating that Zach would bound in that direction.

But Zach had gone right. He bent at the knees as a reverse swing threatened to reduce his mouth to pulp. The club whizzed overhead, and before the warrior could pull back and set himself, Zach streaked the Bowie in a tight arc that opened the warrior's thigh.

The warrior drew away again, pumping his leg a few times as if to assure himself he had not been severely hurt. Then he did a strange thing. He looked at Zach and grinned. Not a friendly grin, by any stretch. It was another expression of defiance, tinged with a degree of respect from one warrior to another.

Zach did the same, then, on an impulse, threw back his head and vented a Shoshone war whoop. The warrior took a bound, thinking to catch him unawares, but Zach sidestepped and thrust.

Gleaming brightly in the sunlight, the Bowie pierced the man's shoulder and he instantly retreated. Now he bore three wounds, but none slowed him down. Circling anew, he sought an opening. He feinted several times, then, in a completely unforeseen move, he held the club horizontal, close to his chest, and speared it outward as if it were a lance.

The club struck Zach in the sternum. There wasn't enough force behind the blow to do much harm, but there was enough to accomplish the warrior's goal, which was to knock Zach off balance. Zach stumbled, attempted to recover, and slipped on slick stones underfoot. His left leg buckled and he fell onto his knee.

Howling, the warrior closed in for the kill.

The war club swished down, connecting with Zach's right wrist. Total torment racked him, and his arm went numb from his fingers to his wrist. Losing his grip on the hilt, he saw the Bowie drop into the water. He lunged to reclaim it with his other hand, but the warrior kicked at his arm, then delivered another brutal swing.

Zach threw himself back, narrowly escaping injury, and sprawled onto his back. Water flowed up over him, as high as his neck, as he scrambled rearward to gain room to rise.

The Sioux, though, had other ideas. Towering above him, the Oglala whisked the club down with deadly might.

A twist of Zach's neck saved him. The war club missed by a sliver's width, splashing water onto his face, into his eyes, and everything blurred. Blinking rapidly, Zach desperately levered upright. His vision cleared just as the club stroked toward his chest.

Shifting, Zach bore the brunt on his shoulder instead, feeling the jolt clear down in his toes. The agony was enough to cause him to grit his teeth to keep from crying out. Stunned, he swayed as if drunk.

Out of the corner of an eye, Zach glimpsed the warrior hiking the war club for the final blow. If it landed, he was done for. He knew it and the warrior knew it.

Most men would have died then and there. Most would have been so overcome by pain that they would be easy prey. But Zach refused to give up, to allow the agony to beat him. Life was too precious—*Louisa* was too precious—for him to stand there while his brains were being splattered. Delving deep within himself, he gathered the energy he needed to spring, to ram into the Sioux's midriff.

Both of them went down. The club glanced off Zach's back as he rolled and flicked a punch that rocked the warrior's jaw.

One-handed, the Sioux looped the club up and in.

Zach blocked it with his right arm, erecting a mental wall against the anguish. His arm was temporarily useless anyway from the previous blow to his wrist. It was a last-ditch tactic, and it left the Oglala open, unable to dodge when Zach punched him where it would hurt the most. A dirty trick by white standards, but Zach was fighting for his life.

In the wilderness there were no rules. It was every man, or woman, for themselves. Survival didn't necessarily always go to the fittest; it went to the cleverest, the quickest, or the most ruthless.

Uttering strangled gasps, the warrior doubled over. He dropped the club, snatched at it, but missed.

Zach hurtled forward like a battering ram, bowling the Oglala over. Raining punches with his left fist, he sought to render the man unconscious. It was now or never. But the Sioux bucked, flinging him off, and he was pitched onto his hip. His outstretched left hand closed on a fist-sized rock.

The Sioux shot upright, shaking his head to clear it. He had reclaimed the war club, and as he reached his full height he streaked it in a vicious curve. Triumph lit his glittering dark eyes.

It was premature.

Zach smashed the rock against the man's knee. A terrible crackling stiffened the warrior like a board, his mouth agape. Then Zach hit the other knee and the warrior folded like an accordion, his head snapping low enough for Zach to deliver a roundhouse that left the Sioux as flat as a pancake.

Panting from the tremendous toll of their exertions, Zach rose unsteadily. Flowing water partially covered the stunned Oglala's face and he sputtered, on the verge of reviving.

Zach picked up the war club. The handle was slippery, but he gripped tighter and raised it above him. He saw the warrior look up. Their eyes locked, and for a fleeting second the Sioux's mirrored the same defiance as before. Zach brought the club crashing down.

The stream blushed scarlet as Zach shuffled to the north bank, retrieving the Bowie as he went. He sank onto his stomach, too tired to do more than lie there gulping breaths. His right forearm tingled with prickling pangs and his shoulder throbbed like the beat of a Shoshone drum. But he would recover. He would live.

A snort from one of the dead Sioux's mounts reminded Zach of his own, which in turn reminded him of Louisa's plight. Willing his body to sit up, he wiped the Bowie clean on some weeds and shoved it into its beaded sheath. His legs balked, but he gained his feet anyway and gathered up the Hawken and his pistols.

Zach dragged the warrior out of the stream but left the rest where they had fallen. Scavengers would dispose of the remains. In another month little would be left except for a few bleached bones, which would ultimately be gnawed down to nothing.

Wearily, Zach walked around the bend to the bay and the mare. He climbed onto the former and led the latter off through the trees, heading northeast, toward the Sioux village. Now he had to save Lou. His plan was to swing wide and come on the village from the north. Locating Lou among all those lodges would be like finding the notorious needle in a haystack, but he wouldn't rest until she was safe in his arms.

Presently, Zach reached the tree line and drew rein. He was thinking of the other four Sioux, the four who had gone east, the four who would undoubtedly spot the wagon train. One or two would stay to keep watch while the others raced for reinforcements. It would be too late in the day for the Sioux to mount a full-scale attack, but come dawn the settlers were in for the fight of their lives.

Zach started to prod the bay but hesitated, swamped by thoughts of Orville Steinmuller and Tommy Baxter and the Quakers. By images of the women who had treated him so decently, and their laughing, carefree children. He gazed north, then east, then north, then east, and finally, with an angry tug on the reins, he rode eastward.

"Damn me all to hell."

He couldn't do it. Zach couldn't let all those people die. He'd warn them, prepare them to fight back, then make a beeline for the village.

Lou should be all right until then, or so Zach tried to convince himself. A few more hours shouldn't make much of a difference. Yet if that was the case, why did anxiety wash over his heart in a seething wave?

Lou! Lou! Zach wanted to shout her name in peals of thunder that would carry for miles, carry to her ears so she would know he had no choice, that what he was doing he did because he had to and not because he put the welfare of the pilgrims before her own.

He could only pray it wasn't the worst mistake of his life.

Louisa regretted her rash act the second she did it. She regretted it more when the tall warrior snapped her up off the ground and shook her, violently, by the hair. Her scalp flared with pain, and her neck felt as if it were about to be wrenched in half. Lou didn't resist, though. She didn't lift a finger even when he slapped her. But when he drew back his hand to do it again, something happened.

From up out of the wellspring of Lou's being gushed roiling, rampaging resentment. Being manhandled was more than she could bear. So when his arm rose, so did her knee—into his groin.

The tall warrior grunted, then staggered back. Turning shades of red and purple, he clutched at himself.

A low cry was voiced by the heavyset woman, who rose to come to his aid.

Earlier, when Lou and the woman were alone, Lou had availed herself of the opportunity to scan the interior. She'd noticed a bow and quiver hanging on the wall, and beside it a battle shield. Both might be useful, but neither interested her half as much as a stone hammer, or maul, lying near the parfleches.

Winona King owned a similar hammer. Common to many tribes, they were used primarily to crack open bones to get at the sweet marrow. This one was about ten inches long, its wooden handle attached to an egg-shaped stone head by thick sinew binding. It wasn't as lethal as a war club or a tomahawk, but it would suffice.

Lou ran to it, plucked it up. She whirled to confront the heavyset woman, who was lumbering toward her with the cane upraised.

"Stay back!" Lou said, but she wasted her breath.

The Sioux woman was beside herself. Cheeks puffing in indignation, she lashed the cane at Lou's face.

Lou winced as it glanced off her cheek. In retaliation, she swept the maul against the woman's jaw. Lou thought it would make the woman back off, but it did more. The woman folded like wet laundry, collapsing in a wheezing heap at Lou's feet.

Amazed at the outcome, Lou stood staring down at the unconscious form when she should have been thinking about her other adversary. Granite fingers wrapped around her wrist as another hand constricted like an iron band on her throat.

The tall warrior was as livid as the woman had been. Locking his leg behind Lou's, he tripped her, throwing her to the ground with him on top. No hint of mercy or compassion was to be found anywhere on his contorted face.

Lou raked her nails across his arm, but it had no effect. She arched her spine to fling him off, but he was much too heavy. Her wrist slipped free, though, and before the tall warrior could seize it again she pounded the maul against his temple, twice. At the second blow, he sagged.

Kicking him off, Lou pumped onto her knees, then walloped him again for good measure. He fell like a poled ox.

Lou slowly stood and backed toward the entrance, but caught herself and halted. She didn't dare show herself outside. The other Oglalas would swarm over her before she went fifty yards.

The other Oglalas! Lou looked at the unconscious warrior, then at the woman. What had she done? If visitors showed up at the lodge, her life was forfeit. She had to lower the flap so no one would barge on in. But as she turned toward the entrance, another shadow fell across it.

Someone was entering!

Chapter Ten

Zachary King was just asking for trouble. He might as well have a sign painted in the Sioux tongue on his chest and on his back, proclaiming, "Here I am! Kill me!" But he didn't care.

Time and again, his pa and his uncle Shakespeare had warned him about letting emotion overcome him in the heat of conflict. There was no surer way of earning an early grave than to lose one's head when one's life was at stake.

"Always keep your wits about you," his pa had advised, "and you'll more than likely keep your hide."

"Be like a rock or be worm food" was how Shakespeare McNair summed it up.

Zach had always tried to do as they taught him. When he'd gone on raids with the Shoshones and in the thick of battle contested with his enemies, he'd always tried to hold his emotions in check.

But it wasn't always easy. It was one thing to be taught what was right, and another to *do* the right thing every time a situation arose in which it had to be done.

As Zach was finding out for himself.

The wise thing to do as he headed east to warn the settlers about the Sioux was to move slowly, to proceed cautiously, to make as little noise as possible. His Hawken should always be ready for instant use. He should always be alert for sign of the other four warriors, and never, ever expose himself.

Those were the precautions Zach *should* take. Instead, he flew pell-mell through the brush, making more noise than a herd of buffalo, virtually inviting a lead ball to the head or an arrow to the chest. To make matters worse, he hadn't taken the time to reload the Hawken or his pistols.

No seasoned frontiersman would do as Zach was doing. No experienced warrior would commit so many unforgivable oversights.

But Zach couldn't help himself. All he could think of was Louisa. Of Lou in the clutches of the Sioux, of what they might be doing to the love of his life at that very second. He had to reach the wagon train quickly so he could hasten to help her. Nothing else was of any consequence.

His heart was awash with worry, it felt as if it were so heavy, it would sink down through his body. His mind was in an anxiety-induced daze, a daze so potent he felt partly numb.

It was panic, plain and simple. Panic that the woman who was everything to him would perish before he got to her. Panic that the bond they shared would be severed for all time. That if he was delayed a second longer than need be, Lou would pay a ghastly price for his tardiness.

I'm coming, Lou! Zach thought over and over again. *I'm coming!*

A wall of brush reared before him, but Zach didn't veer to either side. He plowed into it like a bull gone berserk, heedless of the limbs that tore at his buckskins and tried to gouge his eyes. The bay and the mare were already covered with scratches and cuts. Now they acquired more.

By Zach's reckoning, he wasn't more than half a mile from the wagon train. Undoubtedly, the Sioux had long since reached it and might have already sent one or two men racing to the village. Or so Zach thought until he burst into a clearing and beheld four horses tied to bushes along its fringe.

Abruptly reining up, Zach brought the bay and the mare to a sliding halt. The four Sioux mounts shied, but none broke free.

Rising in the stirrups, Zach scanned the area but didn't see the warriors. About to ride on, he paused.

Stumbling on the mounts had been the best thing that could have happened to him. It had given him a moment to think, to realize what he was doing, to appreciate the monumental blunder he was making. Rushing to save Lou was all well and good, but what help could he be to her dead?

Climbing down, Zach took the bay and mare into the undergrowth and hid them in the deep shadow of an overspreading oak. Then, although the delay rankled him, he reloaded the Hawken and both flintlocks.

When Zach advanced several minutes later, he did so with a clear head, in full control of his faculties, and as carefully as if he were walking on eggshells.

A shudder racked him at how reckless he had been. How stupid. The Sioux could easily have picked him off, and where would that have left Louisa?

Love made people do strange things, Zach decided. Things they wouldn't ordinarily do. He had to remember that so he wouldn't make the same mistake in the future.

It struck him that the woodland was remarkably quiet. Unnaturally so. No birds were singing, no squirrels were chattering, hardly so much as an insect stirred.

The drone of voices fluttered on the sluggish air, punctuated by the pounding of a hammer or mallet. Soon the laughter of children arose, and the low nickering of horses.

Zach angled toward the open prairie. The canvas cover of a Conestoga served as a beacon that drew him to within fifty yards of the wagon train.

Even though it wasn't noon, when they routinely took their midday break, the farmers had stopped. Zach understood why when he saw that the wagon belonging to Jonathan and Tamar Mathews, the Quakers, was tilted, as if the left side had sunk into a hole. But it was the front wheel at fault. They had hit a deep rut, busting several spokes.

Every member of a wagon train carried spare parts. It was required. But repairing a wheel was never easy. The wagon had to be jacked up, the wheel removed. Then the iron rim and the felloes, the outer curved sections, had to be removed so the broken spokes could be extracted and new spokes installed.

One man working alone could do the job in half an hour. Four men, as was the case now, could do it in half that time. Only, Matthews and those helping him weren't in any hurry. They were chatting and joking instead of concentrating on their work.

Where were the Sioux? was the question uppermost on Zach's mind. Stealthily slinking closer, he finally spotted a lone warrior beside a tree, pressed flat against the trunk. A lance was propped next to him.

Some of the women were stretching their legs. Their offspring in tow, they strolled along the tree line. Elizabeth Baxter and Molly Mills were close enough to the tree the warrior was behind for him to leap out and seize them before they could so much as utter a peep.

Zach wanted to shout a warning, but to do so would alert the other three Sioux, some of whom might light a shuck, and he'd rather they didn't. Setting down the Hawken, Zach drew the Bowie and crept forward.

The warrior's back was to him, and the man was concentrating on the women and children to the exclusion of all else. Not once did the Sioux glance over his shoulders. He appeared fascinated by Elizabeth Baxter, by her winsome figure and undeniable beauty. Maybe he entertained the notion of claiming her for his own, for when she sashayed nearer, he tensed as if about to pounce.

By then Zach was only a few feet from the tree. He saw the warrior start to move around the trunk, and a swift stride placed Zach behind him. Clamping his left hand over the Sioux's mouth, Zach buried the Bowie below the man's ribs, not once but twice, sinking the keen steel in to the hilt. He struck so fast that the warrior couldn't react, couldn't fight back or cry out.

Dead on his feet, the Oglala crumpled, his body breaking into convulsions.

Stooping, Zach looped his arm around the Sioux's chest and dragged the limp body into weeds. The slight noise he made was drowned out by the giddy squeals of Susie Mills, who was being swung around and around by her mother.

Elizabeth, watching, chuckled heartily, unaware of the plight she had narrowly escaped.

Zach wiped the Bowie clean on the Sioux's leggings, then rose and raked the vegetation for the remaining three. Since the wagons were strung out over hundreds of yards, the warriors could be anywhere along the line, observing the whites.

"Do it again, Ma!" Susie Mills cried. "Swing me again!"

"Enough now, girl," Molly said. "You're getting too heavy for me. It hurts my shoulders after a while."

"Ah, Ma," Susie pouted.

"Ah, Ma," Elizabeth Baxter echoed, teasing her friend. "You're old before your time." Laughing, she leaned back against the very tree the warrior had been behind.

Crouching, Zach glided over to it. "Elizabeth!" he whispered. "It's Zach King! Don't make a sound!"

"Oh!" Elizabeth blurted, beginning to rotate. "Land sakes, but you startled me!"

"Don't turn around!" Zach commanded. "Don't talk! Just listen!"

His tone rooted Elizabeth in place, and she bobbed her chin to signify she would do as he instructed.

"I can't show myself," Zach hurriedly explained. "There are Sioux spying on the wagon train."

Elizabeth was so shocked, she exclaimed, "Sioux!"

"Hush, or they'll catch on that something isn't right."

"Sorry."

"Pay attention. I want you to go down the line and warn everyone, but tell them not to let on that they know. All the men are to arm themselves. And once they fix the wheel, keep heading west. Louisa and I will catch up by dawn, I hope."

"Wait a second," Elizabeth said, but before she could go on, she was distracted by Molly Mills, who was moseying toward the Conestogas.

"Elizabeth? What's keeping you? Are you talking to someone over there?"

Elizabeth motioned for Molly to stay where she was, whispering, "I'll tell you in a second. Wait there."

Molly did no such thing. Unaware of the menace lurking in the greenery, she waltzed back over, little Susie holding her hand. "What in the world has gotten into you? Why do you look so scared?"

"Please, don't talk, just listen," Elizabeth beseeched.

Zach couldn't dally. He had to hunt down the other Sioux or risk becoming their prey. "Quiet!" he whispered as loud as he dared. "Do as I told you, Elizabeth. And do it quickly."

"What about you?" she asked.

"I'll deal with the warriors who are spying on you, then I have to go after Lou." Assuming that was the end of it, Zach gripped the lance and padded off.

"Wait!" Elizabeth said. "Where's Louisa? Why isn't she with you?"

An answer was on the tip of Zach's tongue, but the sight of a brawny warrior threading through the trees in his general direction goaded him into dropping low and moving to intercept him. The Sioux was glancing every which way, searching, Zach guessed, for the man Zach had just slain.

A prickly bush offered the cover Zach required. Placing the Hawken down, he grasped the lance with both hands and hunkered, bending so low his chin nearly touched the ground. As motionless as a panther, he waited.

The second Oglala was watching Elizabeth, Molly, and Susie hasten toward the wagons. The women repeatedly glanced at the vegetation as if in mortal fear for their lives. It made the warrior suspicious. Taking an arrow from a small quiver on his back, he nocked it to his bowstring.

Zach didn't try to throw the lance. The man was barely in range, and the intervening brush might deflect it.

More alert than ever, the Sioux slanted toward the tree where the dead warrior had been standing. It was obvious he was perplexed by his friend's absence.

Sweat caked Zach's palms, but he couldn't wipe them off, not when any movement, however slight, was bound to be seen. Peering through the bush, he saw the Sioux take one slow step after another.

Zach would have done the same. Caution and survival went hand in hand. Those who rushed in where fools feared to tread, as the old saying had it, were not the ones who lived to a ripe old age.

The warrior was on the other side of the shoulder-high bush, his gaze on the trees bordering the prairie. Cupping a hand to his mouth, he whispered the same word several times.

Zach dug his soles into the soil. Then, when the Oglala took another step, Zach whipped up and around, throwing all his weight-into an upward thrust. The tip of the lance speared into the warrior's abdomen above the navel.

Gasping, the man dropped thc bow, his dark eyes growing to the size of saucers. He took hold of the lance and feebly tried to back away, but Zach held onto it and levered the point in deeper.

Scarlet gushed from the Sioux's mouth. Froth rimmed his lips. Sputtering, he would have fallen were it not for Zach's hold on the haft.

With a sharp twist, Zach pushed the man onto the ground and pinned him there while he thrashed and wheezed like a fish impaled on a harpoon.

It took a god-awful time for the warrior to die.

Finally, Zach wrenched the lance out and traded it for the bow and quiver. With the Hawken in his left hand, he stalked eastward. The final two warriors had to be there, somewhere.

A commotion broke out at the wagons. Settlers were running back and forth, the men arming themselves, the women gathering up their children like frightened hens gathering their broods and scurrying into the Conestogas.

Inwardly, Zach swore. Elizabeth had let him down. The Ohioans were doing precisely what he didn't want them to do. The last two Sioux would realize the whites knew they were being spied on, and would get out of there.

Sure enough, a thicket rustled, and into view they came, side by side, one carrying a war club, the other a rifle.

The pair spotted Zach at the same instant he spotted them.

Louisa May Clark's breath lodged in her throat. She'd forgotten about the open flap! Any Oglala who wanted to enter the lodge could do so. Only if it were closed would visitors stay away.

In a desperate bid Lou darted to the entrance, standing

to one side so whoever was outside wouldn't glimpse her, and let the flap down. Butterflies churned her stomach as footfalls stopped right in front of the flap. Fearing a head would poke in, she elevated the heavy maul.

Anxious seconds passed. The visitor, if indeed it was one and not someone out for a stroll, walked off to the south.

Lou eased onto her knees and gave silent thanks for her deliverance. A groan from the heavyset woman impressed on her that she was being premature. She wasn't out of danger yet, not by a long shot. Death, or worse, awaited her if she was recaptured.

A coil of rope and strips cut from a blanket bought Lou valuable time to think, to plan. She tied the pair, binding their wrists, their ankles, then gagged them.

The woman revived as Lou was knotting her gag and immediately attempted to sit up. Lou pushed her onto her back, but the woman resisted, kicking and struggling. As big as she was, holding her down was like trying to hold down a she-bear.

Suddenly the woman surged up off the ground, sending Lou tumbling. She tried to shout for help, the gag stifling her outcries but not entirely smothering them.

Anyone walking by might hear.

Lou snatched up the maul. She honestly had no desire to hurt the woman, yet she had to be silenced. Brandishing the maul in her face would do the trick, Lou reckoned. But to her consternation, the woman shouted more loudly.

"Some folks just won't learn," Lou said, and walloped her on the temple. Lou didn't use all her strength for fear she would crack the woman's skull.

Moaning, the Oglala oozed onto her side.

Lou moved to the flap to listen. Evidently no one had heard the commotion, so if all went well, she could hide out until sunset, then make a bid for freedom.

In case visitors showed up, Lou armed herself. She took the bow and quiver down from the wall and slung the quiver over her back. She also helped herself to the tall warrior's knife, a fine bone-handled weapon.

The stew's aroma had her stomach growling nonstop. Removing the pot from the tripod, Lou treated herself, but she didn't overdo it. Too much food would make her sluggish. To wash it down, she filled a gourd with water from a water skin.

The feeling of being watched spoiled her idyllic moment. Lou glanced around and saw that the tall warrior had revived and was glaring at her. Grinning, she used sign language to say, "Good food. I thank you."

If looks could kill, the tall warrior's would have shriveled her where she knelt.

"Question. You hungry?" Louisa signed, smiling when the warrior turned beet red and strained against his bounds. She patted the knife hilt and wagged a finger to make him desist. He did, but his eyes were like twin torches.

Lou was enjoying herself immensely. She stepped to the pile of parfleches to examine the contents. In one was a handful of jerked buffalo meat. As she lifted the flap of the next, a scuffling noise warned her that someone was again outside the lodge. Since the flap was down, she figured whoever it was would go away.

Only this time they didn't.

A man called out, as if requesting entry.

Lou dashed to the bow, notched a shaft, and trained it on the entrance. She accidentally scraped the arrow against the quiver as she pulled it out, and the Oglala outside must have heard. He called out again.

Lou had to act, and act quickly, before the man suspected something was wrong and either barged on in or fetched others. Sidling to the right, against the wall, Lou pressed her mouth against her forearm and said in English, "Come on in." The words were so badly distorted, no one could possibly tell what she'd said. But to the man outside, it might, just might, sound as if someone were bidding him to enter.

Her gambit worked. The flap parted. A lean warrior entered and took a stride. Belatedly, he saw the pair she had trussed up and stopped cold.

"Not a sound," Lou whispered. English was so much Greek to him, but the arrow pointed at his heart should guarantee that he got the general idea.

The warrior swung toward her but did nothing rash. He was middle-aged, his eyebrows thick and bushy, his nose broad and flat. A lantern jaw lent him a bulldog aspect.

"What's that you've got there?" Lou asked, excited by the objects he had brought with him: her rifle and both pistols. To give to the tall warrior, was her guess. Wagging the bow, she nodded at the ground. "Put them down." When he didn't obey, she made a show of sighting along the shaft. "I won't tell you again."

Resentfully, the Sioux stooped and deposited the guns at his feet.

"Step back," Lou said, jerking her arms to illustrate. He obeyed, his posture that of a bobcat poised to spring. Easing forward, Lou slowly dipped low enough to pick up a flintlock. But to do so, she had to take her fingers from the arrow, which might be just what the warrior was counting on. Changing her mind, she indicated he should move toward the fire.

The man glanced at the tall warrior, then complied, backing away on the balls of his feet.

Lou pivoted, keeping the arrow trained on him. It put her back to the flap. When something thumped against it, she instinctively spun to confront whoever was coming in. And the moment she did, the lantern-jawed warrior rushed her.

Zach King didn't bother with the bow. The Sioux had seen him, so stealth was no longer essential. Releasing it, he brought up the Hawken, thumbed back the hammer, and fired from the hip.

At the blast the Sioux holding the Kentucky rifle was

spun around, his left shoulder cored. Staggering, he reached out and grasped the slim bole of a cottonwood to keep from buckling.

The other warrior had to get in close for his club to be effective. To that end, he sprang, his club descending in a vicious arc.

Zach had stabbed a hand to a pistol. He was leveling it when the club swished down, and to save himself he threw himself to the right. The war club smashed against the pistol instead, jarring the gun loose. Before he could grab the other one, the warrior was on him like a Viking berserker, blistering the air with blow after blow.

Dancing right and left, Zach kept half a step ahead. Twice his face was nearly bashed in. He tried to unlimber the second flintlock and was clipped on the wrist.

The first Oglala was leaning against the cottonwood, a dark stain spreading across his buckskin shirt. Gamely, he lifted the Kentucky one-handed, his arm shaking as he tried to hold it steady enough to shoot.

All this Zach saw over the other warrior's shoulder. Continuing to retreat, he contrived to spoil the first man's aim by positioning the second man between them. It worked, but it wouldn't for long.

Suddenly, Zach's foot caught in a rut. Thrown off balance, he was easy pickings for the Sioux with the club, who leaped in to administer a killing stroke. But as the club whistled downward, three shots rang out, one after the other, and at each retort a hole blossomed in the warrior's chest, jolting him onto his heels. After the third shot, he deflated like a punctured bubble.

The warrior with the rifle straightened and swiveled toward the source of the gunfire. He shouldn't have. Three more resounded through the woodland, and he died where he stood, riddled by bullets.

As Zach stood, settlers surrounded him. Orville Steinmuller, still bandaged. Steven Mills, Tommy Baxter, Silas Kern. And the Lattigore brothers, none too pleased they'd helped pull his fat out of the fire.

"Are you all right?" Orville asked, scouring the undergrowth. "How many more of the rascals are there?"

"Those were the last," Zach said, "but there's a whole village a couple of miles north of here. While I'm gone, head west. Push your teams until they're ready to drop."

"Elizabeth warned us, just like you wanted," Tommy Baxter praised his wife.

No, Zach reflected, she hadn't, but it would be silly to quibble with men who had just saved his life. "If I haven't caught up with you in, say, two days, you'll have to fend for yourselves."

"Where are you going?" This from Silas Kern.

"After Lou," Zach said. "The Sioux have her."

"Then she's a goner," Todd Lattigore remarked. "You'll only get yourself rubbed out, so why bother?"

"Why bother?" Wes mimicked.

Zach didn't dignify their sneers with a reply. "Remember, cover as many miles as you can," he instructed Steinmuller, and made for his horses.

"Hold on!" Tommy Baxter hollered. "Take a couple of us with you."

"Thanks, but no," Zach responded. Louisa was his fiancée. This was his to do, and his alone. Besides which, the settlers would need every gun they could muster if the Sioux paid them a visit.

"Isn't there anything we can do?" Orville Steinmuller asked.

Zach never broke stride. "Reach the Rockies alive." Because if he couldn't save Lou, if the two of them perished, it would be nice if they didn't die in vain.

Chapter Eleven

When Louisa May Clark heard a noise and turned toward the flap, she inadvertently relaxed the tension on the bow string. Not much, no more than half an inch, yet it made all the difference in the world when the warrior suddenly leaped at her. She released the shaft, but it only sheared a few inches into the man's chest instead of completely through his body, as it would have done if she'd had the string all the way back.

The lantern-jawed warrior was on Lou before she could snatch another arrow. He tried to encircle her with his powerful arms, but the jutting shaft hampered him, so he contented himself with ripping the bow from her grasp and tossing it aside.

When Lou grabbed for the bone-handled knife, a clubbed fist caught her on the cheek. Rocked backward, her vision briefly swam, and her stomach churned. As things came into focus again, she saw the warrior wrench the arrow out and fling it toward the back of the lodge. Lou lowered her hand again, and as she drew her knife, the man drew his own.

The warrior was next to her pistols and rifle, but he made no effort to resort to them. Maybe he was unsure they were loaded. Or maybe he'd never used a gun before. Firearms were hard for tribes like the Sioux to come by. Whites wouldn't trade with them, so they either obtained guns in trade with other tribes or they pried weapons from the rigid fingers of whites they had slain.

Regardless, the warrior slowly moved toward her, his knife held low. A stain was spreading across his buckskin shirt, but he seemed impervious to the wound. It'd had no effect other than to make him angry.

Over by the fire the tall warrior was urgently trying to say something, but his words were muffled by his gag. Excitedly pumping his arms and shoulders, he tried to get the attention of the newcomer.

Lou figured he wanted the lantern-jawed warrior to cut him loose, but the man only had eyes for her. His knife blade gleamed as he shifted, holding it higher. He was going to kill her. Murderous intent radiated from him like heat from the sun. Why he didn't shout for help, Lou couldn't say. Unless he wanted the privilege all to himself.

By the fire, the tall warrior was practically beside himself. He began wriggling toward them while attempting to spit out the gag.

When the attack came, it was so swift that Lou was nearly caught flat-footed. Nine inches of gleaming steel arced at her throat with dazzling speed. She parried, deflecting it more by chance than design.

The Oglala delivered slashes and thrusts without cease, pressing her, seeking to overwhelm her and end the fight quickly.

Lou retreated under his onslaught, countering, parrying, blocking, always on the defensive because he never gave her a breather. She couldn't attack. Which was just as the wily warrior wanted it.

Suddenly the man lunged straight at her heart. Lou leaped to the left to save herself, and as she did, the man sliced at her wrist. A stinging sensation shot up her arm. Blood flowed, but only a little. The cut wasn't deep, but it served notice that unless she came up with a way to win, soon, she would never set eyes on Zach again.

Grinning, the Oglala pressed her with increased vigor. His knife flicked and twisted like a thing alive, like a serpent of glittering metal.

Tiring rapidly, Lou parried another thrust, then skipped backward to avoid a lancing strike at her jugular. Fear spiked into her as she bumped into something and tripped. She flailed her arms in a bid to stay upright, and fell.

The tall warrior who owned the lodge was to blame. He had rolled up against the backs of her legs. And when she toppled, he tried to pin her with the lower half of his body so his friend could finish her off.

Lou had only one recourse; she stabbed him. She plunged the knife into his calf, eliciting a muffled yelp, then flipped to the left and pushed to her feet in time to meet the other man's headlong rush.

The lantern-jawed Oglala was angrier than ever. Showing no mercy, he rained blows like hail.

Compelled to give way, Lou backed against the side of the lodge and her shoulder bumped an object hanging on it. Seconds later, Lou glimpsed the object out of the corner of her eye. A glimmer of hope animated her, motivating her to do as her foe had done moments earlier and spear her knife at his heart.

The Oglala bounded back.

Spinning, Lou grabbed the battle shield and hastily slung it over her left forearm. Now she could hold her own! Elevating it, she waited for the lantern-jawed Sioux to make the next move.

Growling, the man did just that. He renewed weaving his tapestry of death, only now most of his blows were deflected by the shield. Try as he might, he couldn't break through her guard or batter the shield aside. His mounting frustration made him reckless, and after cutting down low to force her to bend, he rammed into her, slamming his shoulder against the shield to bowl her over.

It almost worked. Lou tottered wildly, but she stumbled against the shield's side again and steadied herself.

The lantern-jawed Sioux discarded all caution. Fiercely slicing and hacking, he flew at her with the ferocity of a wolverine. With his other hand he smashed at the shield, hammering it, relying on sheer brute force to succeed where skill hadn't.

Lou retreated, or tried to, but he glued himself to her, relentless as an avalanche, cutting, pounding, slicing, slamming. He was a lot bigger and a lot heavier, and the best she could hope to do was stave off the inevitable for another minute or two. Ever so slowly, Lou bent at the knees.

Thinking she was on the verge of collapse, the Oglala redoubled his attack.

But Lou had intentionally dipped down, the shield against her shoulder to ward him off. He hiked his knife, holding it in both hands, about to try to drive it *through* the shield. But Lou had the opening she had been waiting for. She stabbed up underneath the shield, between his legs, and sank the blade into his groin.

For a moment the tableau was frozen as the warrior's features rippled in astonishment mingled with agony. Then Lou yanked her knife out. Crimson spurted as the Oglala moved to the left, clutching himself and gurgling like a stuck pig.

Just as he had done with her, Lou didn't give him a second's respite. Not when he might cry out, bringing others. She couldn't allow that. He looked up, snapping his arms higher to defend himself, but her knife was already flashing at his throat. It cleaved his flesh with ridiculous ease, severing half his neck.

Teetering, his head flopping at an alien angle, the warrior gurgled as blood poured out of him like water from a fountain. His chest and back were coated red when he sank onto his belly and shook as if cold.

Lou stepped back in case he made a last-ditch attempt to slay her. She was sore from head to waist and bore half a dozen nicks that stung like bee stings. In need of rest, she went to sit. But a sound at the entrance reminded her of the noise she had heard right before the warrior attacked her, and she pivoted, afraid someone else was entering.

Bleeding profusely from his calf, the tall warrior had snaked to the flap and was pushing against it with his forehead. In another moment or two, he would be outside where other Sioux would spot him.

Lou's legs moved of their own accord. She took a step and jumped, landing with her knees bent on the tall warrior's back. Discarding the shield, she gripped his braids to drag him back inside, but he fought her, bucking and kicking. Dislodged, Lou pitched onto her face. When she raised it, his head was all the way out the flap and he was bunching his legs to lever himself the rest of the way.

"You brought this on yourself," Lou said, lancing her blade into his ribs.

The tall warrior stiffened, exhaled loudly, then went as limp as a wet rag. Quickly, Lou rose and hauled him inside. She placed his body next to the other one, then plopped down to catch her breath.

Two dead Oglalas! Lou could forget being adopted into the tribe. They'd torture her for days on end, doing things to her she'd never conceived, even in her worst nightmares. Escape was more crucial than ever.

Willing her weary limbs to move, Lou reclaimed her guns. All three were still loaded. She wedged the pistols under her belt and sat facing the flap, the rifle in her lap. Now all she could do was wait.

But what *about* that sound she'd heard? Curious, Lou parted the flap a fraction. Over near the grass several boys were playing with what appeared to be a ball of cord or twine. Was that the answer? Lou wondered. Had one of them thrown it and it hit the flap by accident? No one else was anywhere near the lodge.

Sitting up, Lou glanced at the sky through the vent at the top. Sunset wouldn't occur for hours yet. Plenty of time for the Sioux to find out what she had done. Plenty of time for them to commence torturing her.

The Comanche trick had worked once; it would work again. Zach switched horses twice, from the bay to the mare and back again, in order to arrive at the small hills bordering the Oglala village faster. By his best reckoning, it was four P.M. when he reined up a mile off.

Zach half expected to find the area swarming with Sioux searching for the eight warriors who had been slain. Needless worry, since the other Oglalas were unaware of their fate. Toward sundown was when family and friends of the dead men would begin to wonder. Searchers might be sent out, or the Oglalas might wait until morning.

Zach needed to hide the bay and the mare. But where, in all that vast grassland, could he conceal animals their size? The grass wasn't anywhere near high enough, and the small hills were too barren. He roved eastward, knowing from experience that flatland was seldom as flat as it seemed. Rain and wind had a habit of carving plenty of gullies and washes.

In due course the bay raised its head and sniffed a few times, as it was wont to do when water was near. Zach was inclined to think the horse was rattled from being ridden so hard, but thirty yards later they came to a small bubbling stream that flowed from north to south.

A stream that must, Zach deduced, pass close by the Sioux village. He should have thought of it sooner. All those Oglalas and their animals needed a lot of water, and the Platte was too far off.

Climbing down from the bay, Zach allowed the two horses to quench their thirst. Cupping his hands, he treated himself to a few sips. After a while, he walked the pair into the grass and ground-hitched them.

Unlike the Platte, the stream wasn't flanked by vegetation. But the channel was below the level of the adjacent ground, so anyone moving along it might elude detection.

Zach hunkered, facing north, to await the advent of night. Looking for Lou in a village that size was akin to looking for the proverbial needle in a haystack, but he refused to be discouraged. Somehow or other he would find her. Somehow or other he would save her.

Lou's image floated before him, as intangible as ether. Zach imagined her smiling in that affectionate, playful way she had, imagined her loving gaze, and grew warm inside, as if a fire had been lit in his heart.

"Lou, Lou," Zach said softly, his throat constricting. More than ever he realized just how much she meant to him, and how devastated he would be should harm befall her. "I love you so much."

Zach heard a horse nicker. Preoccupied with thoughts of Louisa, he thought it was the bay or the mare. Then it dawned on him that the nicker had come from the northwest, not the east. Rising slightly, he spied a knot of warriors a long way off, moving northward toward the village. They hadn't spotted him, but they might spot his horses.

Zach trained the Hawken on them. There were four in all, which was more than enough to do him in. But they never deviated from their course. Within minutes they had dwindled to specks.

Sitting back down, Zach tried to picture Lou's image again, but his mood had been spoiled.

Apprehension ate at him like an acid. His mouth went dry and he broke out in a cold sweat. Was this what love did to a person? Zach mused. Turned them into miserable wrecks? He had to be strong, had to remember he was a Shoshone warrior, remember he had counted coup in hand-to-hand combat. The Sioux were formidable, true, but no more so than the Blackfeet or the Bloods, and he had bested both at one time or another.

Being strong was difficult, though. For no matter how Zach tried, he couldn't shake a nagging dread that he was already too late, that Louisa had suffered a fate worse than death, or death itself.

Please let her be alive! Zach pleaded, gazing heavenward. *Great Mystery—the Lord God—whatever, whoever you are, please don't let me lose her before our life together has really begun!* He blinked away welling tears and coughed to clear his throat. *Please! Please!*

Lou didn't mean to doze. She had been sitting for so long in the stifling warmth of the lodge that her chin drooped and her eyes closed, and the next thing she knew, she snapped awake and realized the sun was setting.

Stretching, Lou peeked out the flap. The boys were gone. No one else was within her range of vision. The light was fading rapidly, but it would be another hour yet before it was dark enough for her to make her bid. So she had ample time to prepare.

The heavyset woman, Lou observed, hadn't revived yet. Concerned, Lou checked the woman's pulse and found it strong.

Among the many items lining the lodge wall were several beaded dresses. They were much too big to fit Lou, but she selected one and slipped it over her head. She looked like a human tent, the buckskin drooping in great folds and spilling down over her moccasins.

Taking the woman's cane, Lou reached behind her and slid it under the dress, aligning it across her shoulders. The weight of the garment sufficed to brace the cane against her neck so it wouldn't fall. Now the dress fit a little better, or so it would seem to casual observers. Lou paced back and forth, experimenting. So long as she didn't move too fast or bend down, the deception might succeed.

Impatient, Lou stared at the vent, wishing night would come. From time to time she heard voices, but none came close enough to cause her alarm.

Lou did grow anxious, though, when a man went around the village yelling. She heard him to the northwest, then the south, then the northeast. The Oglala equivalent of a town crier, she reckoned, and grew anxious when he neared the lodge. But he walked on by.

His yelling woke up the heavyset woman, who rolled onto her side and recoiled on seeing the two dead men. Mewing like a kitten, she crawled to the tall warrior and rubbed her head against his in a vain bid to revive him.

"I didn't want to do it," Lou said quietly.

Hatred blazed. Muttering into the gag, the woman shot barbs from her eyes. Had she been free, there would have been hell to pay.

Never in Lou's whole life had night taken so long to descend. Itching to be off, she paced and paced. As soon as it was dark enough, she adjusted the dress and pushed on the flap.

Three women, chattering like chipmunks, were coming up the trail from the stream. Lou would have ducked back, but one looked toward the lodge and waved, so Lou returned the favor, careful not to fully show herself.

Thankfully, the trio blithely strolled off toward their own lodges.

Stepping outside, Lou straightened and hurriedly shoved the Hawken down the front of her bulky dress, then pressed the rifle against the dress to enhance the illusion the dress fit. Confident she could fool most anyone, Lou moved toward the trail, stopping when another woman bustled up it bearing a water skin.

Lou veered to the right so the woman wouldn't get a good look at her. The Oglala, though, hastened northward, showing no interest. Since using the trail was fraught with peril, Lou opted to follow the edge of the encampment until she was far enough south to slip off across the prairie unnoticed.

All went well initially. Most of the Sioux were in their lodges, about to partake of their evening meal. Other than some boys tending horses, a few men engrossed in conversation, and an occasional homeward-bound woman or two, Lou had the village to herself.

She walked at a normal pace to avoid attracting undue attention. Whenever anyone glanced in her direction, Lou averted her face. The same when she passed lodges with open flaps. Which was frequent, since it was Sioux custom to erect tepees so the entrances were toward the rising sun.

Lou had covered over a hundred yards and had only a couple of hundred more to go when the pad of paws announced she had company.

A camp dog was shadowing her, one of many mongrels that earned its keep by alerting the Oglalas when enemies were near. And this particular dog took its responsibility seriously, for it growled as it approached, the hackles on its neck rising.

When Lou shifted toward it, the dog slowed. She smiled, but she didn't say anything. Not when the dog was accustomed to hearing the Sioux tongue. Hearing English might incite it further.

Going on, Lou held to a slow walk. To do otherwise would arouse suspicion. The dog trailed her. Its hackles were down and it had stopped growling, but it wasn't entirely convinced she was who she pretended to be. Again and again it sniffed loudly, turning its head this way and that.

Maybe it was confused, Lou speculated. Her scent was mixed with that of the dress's owner, the heavyset woman, so the dog couldn't tell if she was really an Oglala or not. She wished it would stray off and pester someone else, but it had a mind of its own.

Another lodge with an open flap appeared on her right. Lou came abreast of the opening just as an older man poked his head out. Smiling, he said a few words. She gave a little wave and moved a little faster, hoping he would excuse her bad manners by assuming she was in a hurry to get somewhere.

The man stepped outside and addressed her.

Cloaked in darkness, Lou felt bold enough to look back and wave once more. The dog had halted and was gazing at the old Oglala as if awaiting a command.

Lou walked even faster, her knees occasionally bumping the Hawken's stock. She thought she would make it. She thought she had deceived the old Oglala. But the cane on her shoulders picked that moment to slip. Before she could reach up and realign it, her huge dress folded in on itself like a collapsing tent. Only someone with extremely sharp eyesight would have noticed, and apparently the old warrior had the vision of a hawk. For as she grasped the cane to replace it, the old man shrieked like a demon brought to life.

Lou began to lift the dress off over her head. She had it partway up when she saw the old man point and snap words at the mongrel, which promptly flew toward her, a streak of fur-covered teeth and claws. Lou couldn't possibly get the dress all the way off before the dog reached her. So, curling back the hammer, she shoved the Hawken out from under it and squeezed the trigger when the dog was fifteen feet away.

Nothing happened. Nothing at all, other than a muted click. There was no blast, no cloud of smoke. Lou glanced down but couldn't tell much in the dark. The only explanation she could think of was that the folds of buckskin had somehow prevented the hammer from striking the cap.

In a flurry of paws, snarling savagely, the dog was upon her. Jumping high, it bit at her chest but ripped into the dress instead. Then the mongrel, in a frenzy, clamped hold and whipped from side to side as if to tear her apart.

Lou was tossed like a rag doll in a gale. She couldn't bring the Hawken to bear, couldn't unravel it from the dress. But she still had her pistols. Seizing one, she drew it, shoved the muzzle against the beast, and fired.

Yipping shrilly, the dog tumbled and flopped about like a fish out of water.

The old man was shouting with the gusto of a twenty-year-old while hurrying toward her, both fists upraised.

Tepee flaps from one end of the village to the other were thrown wide and warriors and women spilled out. Dogs began braying in a raucous din. Some of the horses, agitated by the uproar, whinnied and stomped.

Lou didn't want to kill the old man, so she merely pointed the spent pistol at him. When he lurched to a halt, she spun and raced into the high grass, holding the bulky dress up about her waist so she could move more freely. But it wasn't freely enough. The heavy folds hindered her, as did the rifle, which was snagged.

Oglalas were converging on the old man, who was hopping up and down beside the stricken dog.

Lou ran for her literal life. When she was sure they couldn't see her, she stopped and shed the dress, untangling her rifle in the process.

The encampment buzzed with activity. Men were hurrying toward their mounts, and torches were being brought. Five or six people were jogging to the tall warrior's lodge. They ducked inside, and a moment later a piercing wail arose. Two warriors rushed back out, yelling, spreading the news.

They would roast her over a spit! That was Lou's assessment as she sped into the night in long, loping strides. She had always been fleet of foot, and as a girl had won many a race. A cocky little thing, she had challenged every boy who would take her on. Until her mother found out, that was, and made it clear prim and proper young ladies did *not* go around beating the pants off boys. As it were.

But that had been years ago. Lou hadn't done much running in ages. It wouldn't matter if she had, because there wasn't a human being alive who could outrun a horse. And several dozen were being readied to pursue her.

Water splashing around her ankles gave Lou pause. She had reached the stream. Crossing, she paused again, uncertain which direction to take. Should she go east? North? Or south?

The Oglalas probably thought she'd want to get as far from the village as possible, and would go east. So to throw them off, Lou should pick north or south. North, though, would take her deeper into nowhere. South would bring her to the Platte River, and from there finding the wagon train should be child's play.

Lou jogged southward.

The Sioux were rushing to and fro, the flickering glow of scores of torches playing over them as if they were actors on a stage. Riders trotted from all points of the compass to join the growing search party. No one was whooping and yipping, as was customary. To a man, they were as grim as the Reaper.

Lou tore her gaze from the village and sprinted harder. Suddenly a figure reared up in front of her. Scared half out of her wits, she went to scream, but a hand clamped over her mouth as warm lips were pressed to her ear.

"Don't make a sound, my darling. It's me."

Indescribable joy flowed through Lou, joy so pure, so potent, it was as intoxicating as the finest wine. "Zach!" she exclaimed softly, flinging her arms around him. "Oh, sweet Zach! It's really you?" She couldn't credit her own senses.

"They'll be after us in a minute," Zach said, prying her loose. "We can't linger."

Lou wanted to hug him forever, but she nodded. "Lead the way. Where are the horses? Very far?"

"Too far," Zach answered, pulling her after him. "A couple of miles."

The Sioux were almost to the prairie, spreading out along a wide front, every fourth or fifth man holding a torch aloft.

Lou didn't care. She had been reunited with her beloved. Nothing else was of any consequence. At that moment, she was the happiest woman on the planet. "I knew you would come for me."

Zach looked at her, his features mired in gloom. "Only death could keep me away."

"I love you," Lou said huskily, and then there was no more time for endearments.

At a bellow, the Oglalas swept eastward, their torchlight rippling over the grass like molten gold. They were out for blood, and they would not be denied.

Chapter Twelve

Zach King was so choked with emotion, he could barely think straight. Lou was alive she was by his side! His chest felt fit to burst with joy. But he had to contain it. They weren't safe yet. Far from it. They couldn't breathe easy until they eluded the Sioux. And to do that, he needed all his wits about him. By a monumental force of will, he clamped a lid on his feelings and picked up the pace.

Lou was keeping an eye on the Oglalas. Sixty to seventy yards off, spread along a hundred-yard front, they advanced toward the stream. The warriors at the near end of the line were about abreast of Zach and her, and were bound to spot them unless they found cover.

At a glance, Zach realized the same thing. They had only a minute or two in which to act. Halting, he moved to the stream, got down on one knee, and plunge his left arm in. The water was about a foot deep.

A crazy notion Zach had just might work. "Do as I do," he whispered, easing off the bank.

Confused as to what he was up to, Lou nonetheless followed his example.

Zach quickly laid his rifle and both pistols close to the edge and bent blades of grass over them. Then he lowered himself into the chill water and pressed against the side, tilting his head so his nose and one eye were above the surface.

Lou caught on right away. Concealing her own weapons, she sank into the stream, shivering at how cold it was. Her head brushed Zach's feet as she flattened against the dank earthen bank and craned her neck to breathe through her nose. Clamminess spread over her as the water soaked her buckskins. She could see the stars overhead and murky ranks of grass on the other side, but that was all.

Hooves thudded. Presently a rosy glow spread across the grass, spreading toward them.

"Now," Zach whispered, lowering himself underwater.

Taking a deep breath to fill her lungs, Louisa hugged the bottom, her face close to the bank so her pale skin wouldn't give her away.

A pair of riders appeared, the last two in the long line, one holding a torch on high. They were seven or eight yards away, intently scouring the prairie ahead. The water distorted their images, made them appear more like ogres than men.

Loud splashing buffeted Lou as their mounts entered the water. Neither warrior looked down. It didn't occur to them that anyone would hide *in* the stream. Focused on the prairie, they crossed and rode off into the night.

By then Lou's lungs were straining for air, but she steeled herself to stay under as long as Zach did. When he finally deemed it safe and raised his head, so did she. So as not to make any noise, she breathed through her nose.

Zach started to sit up, to get out of there while they

still could, but the drum of more hooves drove him under the water again. "Down!" he whispered as he sank.

Lou didn't have time to take a breath. She ducked under just as another Oglala materialized, galloping to catch up with the others. His mount came right toward her, and she was about to throw herself out of the animal's path to avoid being trampled when the man jabbed his heels and the horse sailed up and over her, vaulting the stream in a fluid hurdle. She saw its legs, its belly, the warrior's moccasins. When it came to earth, she could have sworn the ground shook.

Lou's chest hurt something awful. She knew it was wise to wait a bit before showing herself, but she couldn't go another five seconds without air. Pushing up, she gulped it in.

Zach slowly rose to scan the prairie, water dripping off his buckskins as he palmed his pistols. To the east the line of horsemen were spreading out farther to cover more ground. To the west dozens of Oglalas were gathered around a pair of bodies being taken from a lodge. "Let's go," he whispered, climbing out.

They ran bent at the waist, their moccasins squishing like soggy sponges, their clothes clinging to them like a second, albeit soaked, skin.

Fatigue nipped at Lou, her ordeal taking its toll, but she shrugged it off.

Zach was in the grip of the same feeling he'd experienced back at the Platte: icy, ravaging fear. Not for himself, but for Louisa. He was terrified of being caught, of having her fall into the clutches of the Sioux again. He would gladly give his life to prevent that, even if it meant throwing himself in front of an arrow or lance.

Love and constant fear, Zach was learning, went hand in hand. Suppressed fear that a loved one would perish, fear most people denied until the unthinkable came to pass. He couldn't let it paralyze him, though. For both their sakes.

Over the next half an hour the village and the torches

receded into the distance. Zach's fear lessened but didn't go entirely away. Nor would it, he reflected, for as long as he lived. A kernel had been planted in the soil of his soul that would exist there forever, waiting to sprout whenever the love of his life was imperiled.

Lou was so giddy, she yearned to laugh aloud. She had escaped! She had survived! And best of all, she was reunited with her heart's desire. When they at long last reached the horses, she flung herself at Zach and lavished warm kisses on his lips, his cheeks, his neck. "I love you, I love you, I love you!" she breathed.

Immensely delighted, Zach responded in kind. It was silly of them to be so childish, what with the Oglalas liable to show up at any moment. But holding her and kissing her soothed him. It restored his sense that all was right with the world—even if it wasn't.

They kissed until they were panting with passion, until Lou stepped back, smoothed her shirt, and asked a question that had been bothering her since her capture. "What about the farmers? Do they know about the Sioux?"

"They know," Zach confirmed, turning to fork leather. As they goaded their animals into motion, he briefly detailed his clash at the river, then listened as Louisa related her own life-or-death struggle.

"By tomorrow the Oglalas will be out in force," she declared.

Yes, they would, Zach mused. Not because Lou had escaped, or because of the missing warriors, but because of Mole. The old healer had promised to keep quiet only as long as none of his people were harmed. Now two had been slain. Mole would inform the tribe's leaders, and a war party would be organized.

Or would he tell them? Zach wondered. The other Oglalas wouldn't take kindly to Mole's keeping the presence of the whites a secret. In fact, they might be downright mad. Were Zach in Mole's moccasins, he'd keep his mouth shut.

Time would tell what the healer did. In the meantime, all Zach could do was wait for the Sioux to show but pray they didn't. Hope for the best but prepare for the worst. Not a bad philosophy, when he thought about it. Words of wisdom to live by.

"A penny for your thoughts," Lou said, loudly enough to be heard above the hoofbeats of their mounts.

"I was thinking of how much I love you," Zach fibbed. She had been through so much already that burdening her with an added worry was needless.

"Soul mates," Lou said, and smiled.

They didn't overtake the Conestogas until noon the next day. The settlers had done as Zach directed, and gone him one better. They'd pushed on through the night, refusing to stop except for short breaks. The teams were worn out, the pilgrims exhausted, but they had covered twice as many miles as they would have otherwise.

Orville Steinmuller called a halt when Zach and Lou rode up. Everyone, or nearly everyone, rushed to greet them. Women and children hugged Lou while some of the men clapped Zach on the back. Notably aloof were Frank Jensen and the Lattigore brothers.

Zach was besieged with questions, but holding up his hands, he silenced them and declared, "Time for talk later. Right now we have to keep on going. I know you're worn out, I know your animals are on their last legs. But we'll all be maggot bait if we don't put a few more miles behind us by sunset."

Nightfall saw them camped in a tract of woods, the wagons in a tight circle, the settlers and their stock crammed into the center. Half the men stood guard until two, the other half until dawn. Zach was on the second shift, and hardly had the first faint hint of daylight brightened the eastern sky than he went from wagon to wagon, waking everyone up.

After a hasty breakfast, they hitched up their teams and rolled out.

The morning waxed and waned. So did the afternoon. Zach was glad the Sioux hadn't shown, but he was puzzled by their absence. His puzzlement grew greatly over the next several days, and on the evening of the fourth one he mentioned it to Lou, who was seated between Tamar Mathews and Helen Marsh.

"It's a miracle, that's what it is!" the Quaker woman declared. "The Good Lord is watching over us."

Zach preferred a more logical explanation. The next morning, when he rode to the river to water the bay, one presented itself. In dried mud were buffalo tracks a week or so old. They jarred his memory. He recollected that during his talk with Mole, the old healer had signed that the Oglalas were planning to go on a big buffalo hunt.

There was the answer. The Oglalas had been low on food. They'd needed fresh meat, and had pitched their village near a large herd. They couldn't delay their hunt because the herd would move on.

Zach had once gone on a Shoshone surround, as the whites called it, which had taken the better part of a week. After the warriors stalked and slew as many buffalo as they could, the women had gone out with their sharp knives and travois. They'd skinned the buffalo, butchered the meat, and hauled everything back to the village. Most was hung out to dry, so it could be made into jerky or pemmican. Then a celebration had been held, a grand feast that lasted two whole days alone.

It was possible the Sioux would take just as long.

Zach's hunch was borne out. Another week elapsed and the Sioux still didn't appear. But it wasn't until several days later that Zach let himself believe the worst was over. The wagon train wasn't going to be attacked.

Maybe, when all was said and done, it really was a miracle.

The settlers fell into their old routine. Summer crept along, and so did they. A few wheels had to be repaired, an axle on one of the wagons busted, and the Kern boy broke an arm when he fell from a tree. Otherwise, all went well.

One warm evening amid the sea of grass, Orville Steinmuller, now fully mended, produced a checkerboard and invited Zach to play. Others wanted a turn. One thing led to another, resulting in a heated competition to see who was the best.

Orville was persuaded to set up elimination matches. After two weeks it had boiled down to Frank Jensen and him.

A festive air filled the camp the night of the deciding match. The women had used the last of their meager sugar to bake sweetcakes. A small log was dragged to the middle of the circle, and Orville and Jensen sat down. A hush fell as the game commenced, with everyone hanging on every move.

Jensen was no beginner. He lured Orville in and took several of Orville's pieces early on. Only it turned out that Orville was luring him in, setting him up for a triple jump that crowned a king.

Until the very end the outcome was in doubt. When, late into the night, Orville took the last of Jensen's reds, hearty cheers rewarded his achievement.

Zach had noticed a change come over them since he joined the train. Where before they had been a group of closely knit families, now it seemed as if they were one giant family. Except for the bigot and the Lattigores, who pretty much kept to themselves, everyone was always kind and caring to one another.

Zach began to see his father's people in a whole new light—to see that many were decent and honorable. It was wrong of him, he realized, to think poorly of whites simply because a few thought poorly of him.

Spirits were high. All was well. Then Nature threw a tantrum.

On a muggy afternoon when the drivers were dozing in their seats, a dark column of clouds boiled out of the west, clouds as black as pitch. The wind intensified, gusting hard enough to blow off a hat or bonnet.

A hundred yards ahead of the Conestogas, Zach and Lou appraised the gathering storm, then glanced at each other.

"We're in for it," Lou commented.

Zach hauled on his reins and galloped back. "Make a circle," he instructed Orville. "Get the women and children under the wagons. Tie down everything that isn't already tied down."

Steinmuller gazed at the writhing cloud bank. "Why so nervous over a little rain and thunder?" he asked.

What could Zach say? Those who came from east of the Mississippi had never seen Nature in all its bristling, rampaging fury. Words couldn't describe what they were in for, so all he said was, "You'll find out. Now hurry, Orville. Hurry."

As it was, they were barely battened down when the skies opened, unleashing a deluge of raindrops the size of bullets amid brilliant streaks of lightning and deafening booms of thunder. Crash after titanic crash resounded in continual cannonade. Shrieking wind shook the Conestogas, tearing at the canvas and rattling articles inside.

Crouched under the Steinmullers' wagon next to Lou, Zach stared into the wall of rain, futilely striving to see a bright spot to the west. Instead he saw a vivid blue bolt sizzle down and strike a nearby tree in a bright, seething flash. An acrid odor filled his nostrils as clods of dirt pelted the wagon.

The team whinnied in terror and would have run off, but they were hemmed in by the Conestoga in front of them. Their panicked stamping and rearing made the Steinmuller wagon sway wildly, frightening Agatha, who clutched her husband.

"It will be all right, dear," Orville soothed her.

That remained to be seen, as far as Zach was concerned. The storm's violence was increasing, not slackening. The wind howled like a hurricane, whipping the rain against the wagons in lashing sheets.

Somewhere a child screamed.

Swiveling, Zach surveyed the other Conestogas but couldn't tell where the scream came from. All the wagons were still upright and essentially intact, but that might change. Since the scream wasn't repeated, he figured the child was merely scared.

"It's getting colder," Lou mentioned.

That it was. The drop was slow but steady. Zach crawled to the side of the wagon bordering the circle to assure himself the bay and the mare hadn't broken loose. Someone else's horse had, but catching it would have to wait.

For ten more minutes the storm pummeled them, churning the ground into muddy muck. The canvas cover on Jensen's wagon was torn off and sailed away with the wind, along with his curses.

Shortly thereafter, Agatha Steinmuller cocked her head. "Listen. The rain is slacking off. It's almost over."

Zach didn't have the heart to inform her she was wrong. She would find out soon enough. The raindrops did reduce in size and number, though, from a riotous downpour to a sustained drizzle.

Agatha smiled. "What are we waiting for? Give the signal."

Zach had ordered everyone to stay under their wagons until he told them it was all right. "Not yet."

"Why not, dear boy?" Agatha said. "A little wet never hurt anybody."

"No, but a lot of hail has."

"Hail?"

A minute later it began, a few hailstones no bigger than peas falling at random. Gradually the number grew, and so did their size. From peas to marbles, a barrage that bombarded the wagons like buckshot and soon covered the ground an inch deep. Many of the horses were nickering in pain, but there was nothing that could be done for them.

"This is awful," Agatha remarked.

There were degrees of awful, as the settlers learned when the marbles swelled to the size of walnuts. Now the horses were beside themselves, and the canvas on every wagon was being rent.

Zach watched the hail, only the hail. Walnut-sized was bad enough, but he had seen larger. Hail the size of apples, capable of reducing men and animals to shattered shells. Hail that could reduce the wagons and their contents to rubble.

"Zach!" Lou said.

Zach had seen it. A hailstone twice as big as all the rest. He looked for more but didn't see any. Maybe it was just the one. Maybe the settlers rated two miracles.

A horse was down, a pony belonging to the Marsh family. Jacob Marsh ran out to help it up but was driven back under his Conestoga by the ceaseless hammering of the rocklike ice.

"Stay under cover!" Zach hollered.

No one else tempted fate, and bit by bit the hail tapered off. When it ended, the wind suddenly died, the sky brightened, and shimmering rays of sunlight bathed the white carpet left in the storm's wake.

Zach poked his head out for a look-see. The roiling black clouds were sweeping eastward, bursts of lightning crackling in rumbling cadence. He stepped out and straightened, his feet crunching the hail, careful not to slip.

"Is it over?" Orville inquired. "How much damage was done?"

"See for yourself."

In Zach's opinion, they got off easy. Half the canvases were shredded but could be mended. A mirror in one wagon was shattered; a set of heirloom china in another was lost to posterity. The Jensens had more personal effects broken or ruined than anyone. Charlotte took it stoically, but Frank was fit to be tied.

None of the horses was severely injured, and the pony was its old frisky self by evening. But they had all been badly pelted, and to give them time to recuperate, Zach announced that the train wouldn't move out until the next morning.

That night around the campfires the farmers were as somber as grave diggers. They sipped black coffee or stared into the fire, as bleak as if attending their own wake. An important lesson had been learned that day, a lesson every trapper and mountain man who ventured west before them had also learned: The wilderness was an extremely harsh mistress.

"What have we let ourselves in for?" Orville Steinmuller asked no one in particular, breaking the silence.

To Zach's own mild surprise, he answered, "A life of freedom, of doing as you please, of rearing your families as you see fit. But everything in life has a price. Even freedom isn't free. You pay for it with your blood, your sweat, your tears."

Tamar Mathews looked at him. "How is it, Brother King, that one so tender of years is so worldly wise?"

Zach had never thought of himself that way. Shrugging, he responded, "I reckon I've had a good teacher."

"And who was that? Your father?"

"Life."

The rest of their journey was relatively uneventful. Wolves tried to get at the horses one night and were driven off. Another bear prowled close to camp, but an alert sentry fired at it and the griz crashed off through the brush.

Filling their water skins to bursting, they left the security of the Platte and bore due west. A few days out from the mountains a small heard of buffalo crossed their path. Zach took six farmers with him and brought back enough meat to last all of them for months.

Then came the glorious morning they had all been waiting for. Before them reared rolling green foothills, stretching for as far as the eye could see to the north and south. Beyond, towering to the clouds, were the regal Rockies, spectacular miles-high peaks, many crowned with ivory mantles of snow, breathtaking in their majesty.

The families gathered at the head of the train to gape in wonderment. Orville expressed the sentiments of them all when, with tears trickling down his cheeks, he said throatily, "I had no idea."

Zach pointed to the south. "Bent's Fort is a day's ride. You can stock up on provisions before heading for the high country."

"We're here," Tommy Baxter said in amazement. "We're really here."

Frank Jensen shouldered through the gawkers. "Not yet we're not. I thought we hired King to lead us to a valley higher up. Why's he leaving us so soon?"

Orville dabbed at his eyes with his sleeve. "Our agreement, Frank, was for him to guide us to the mountains, which you'll have to grant he's done, and done admirably, too. He's fulfilled his end of the bargain. Now we fulfill ours. I need your share of the money."

Jensen folded his arms across his chest. "I'm not paying him a cent. As far as I'm concerned, he hasn't earned it."

Two months ago, Zach would have leaped off the bay and thrashed the bigot to a bloody pulp. But those two months had changed him. "Keep your money, Jensen."

"What?"

"I don't want it," Zach said. "I wouldn't take it now if you got down on your knees and begged me to."

Jonathan Mathews turned. "But Brother King, without Brother Jensen's share, we can't raise the hundred dollars we promised. We'll be short."

Zach thought of all he had been through: his fight with Jensen, his fight with the Lattigores, the Pawnees, the

Sioux, the grizzly, the days on end of blistering sun, the hail, the saddle sores. Then he gazed at Lou, who smiled and nodded. "Keep it. Keep it all."

"You can't mean that," Orville said.

"You said yourself that you were low on money," Zach noted. "And you'll need a lot of supplies to see you through until spring. Consider it my gift. Or, rather," he smiled at his fiancée, "*our* gift."

Lou had never been prouder of him than she was at that moment. Reaching for his hand, she gave it a tender squeeze.

Tommy Baxter stepped between their horses. "It wouldn't be fair not to pay you what we owe. A man should always make good on his word."

"Let it be, Thomas," Agatha Steinmuller said.

"But we can't—"

"Let it be."

Zach held his hand out to Orville. "If you ever make it up Long's Peak way, look us up. You're welcome at our table anytime. That goes for most all of you." None of them asked who the exceptions were.

"I'll miss you, son," the older man said.

Zach was taken aback to see Orville misting over again. Agatha, Molly, little Susie and Elizabeth Baxter were also about to cry. A sudden urge to leave spurred him into wheeling the bay. "I wish you the best," he said, and headed for the foothills. Moments later Lou trotted alongside, her mouth curled in one of her knowing smiles. "Don't say a word," he told her.

"I wouldn't think of it."

Zach knew better.

"But have I mentioned lately how adorable you are?"

"I'm a warrior, remember? You make me sound like a rabbit."

"Adorable, adorable, adorable."

Chuckling, Zach said, "Is this what I have to look forward to? Thirty years of you giving me a hard time?"

"If you're lucky, maybe forty years."

Smiling, Zachary King and Louisa May Clark rode on up into the emerald foothills, and into their future together.